Rusty Wilson

Chasing After Bigfoot

My Search for North America's Most Elusive Creature

If you decide to go chasing after Bigfoot, all I can say is to be prepared for anything, because I can pretty much guarantee it won't turn out like you might expect.

You see, I believe those big Bigfoot feet march to the beat of a different drummer, a drummer our human ears can only hear when we are very still and very quiet and very humble.

—Rusty Wilson

• FOR •

Alisha, Chris, Drew, Erika, Jason, Jaymi, John, Kerry, Mojo, Roger, Ursula, and all who have encouraged and helped me.

Without you, this book wouldn't exist.

And for Sarah.

Contents

Foreword

Dear Fellow Adventurers,

As you may know, I'm a fly-fishing guide, and I've collected many Bigfoot stories around campfires from my clients. ("Rusty Wilson's Bigfoot Campfire Stories" and others in that series.)

When I'm sitting around the fire listening to these stories, the storyteller will often tell the actual place where their Bigfoot encounter happened. I almost always change these locations in my books. Given what I believe is the declining number of this species, I feel we need to be very careful to not intrude on their habitat any more than we already do.

But I always wondered what it would be like to go searching in those places, places where there have been actual encounters—some of which were real doozies. I call places where there was more than one such encounter "Bigfoot hotspots."

My wife, Sarah, and I discussed this for some time, and I always felt a bit conflicted about the whole thing—I would hear of others going on organized searches, sometimes in fairly large numbers, and I'd wonder, what does the Big Guy think about all this? I always felt that he or she probably felt hunted. I know I would.

I wanted to see a Bigfoot, but I just couldn't justify intruding into their terrain. I know I wouldn't like someone coming into my territory, purposely searching for me and my family.

While thinking about all this (usually while fishing), a thought finally began to take shape: what if I were to go to Bigfoot hotspots and just hang around camp, trying to be as unobtrusive as possible and not tramping into the woods looking for them? Would they maybe come to me from curiosity?

Another thought was in the back of my mind—would I be able to find definitive proof of the existence of Bigfoot, something many scoff at or question? And if I did, what would I do with it?

I tried to be honest with myself. If I did find such proof, I knew I would never sell it, and I wasn't sure I would even share it with anyone except my wife, who I trust implicitly. I'm not interested in self-aggrandizement, and I feel that most media sensationalize the topic of Bigfoot. I wanted no part of that.

I simply have a life-long curiosity about Bigfoot. I wanted to see one—in a nutshell, meet the elusive creature I'd heard so much about over campfires. I also feel strongly that we must start preserving their habitat, and this won't happen until we can list them as a real species, and possibly as an endangered one.

But what part I wanted to play in that was not clear to me, as I wanted nothing to do with anything that could also possibly make them even more endangered.

So, I decided I would go camping. I would take off for a month and follow my heart, go chasing after the Big Guy—though I can tell you, when I realized my dream could become reality, I was kind of scared.

Did I have what it would take to camp in a tent in these Bigfoot hotspots all alone? I wouldn't actually be chasing after Bigfoot—if anything, he'd be chasing after me. I hoped I had the fortitude and courage to let him find me, were he so inclined. To be honest, the thought was both intriguing and terrifying.

And so, in late July, off I went, and I can tell you this—it takes a lot more to live through a Bigfoot story than it does to hear someone else's. There were times when I amazed myself at my courage—but more often, I was shocked at how big of a chicken I could be. Things just didn't come down like I expected them to—not one bit.

Unlike in my campfire stories, the locations in this book are exactly where the event happened. I mention this because you might want to stay away from those places—or go there, if you're ready. My vision of Bigfoot has always been that he's a benign creature, but there were a few times during my "expedition" that I wasn't so sure.

So, make yourself a cup of hot chocolate, kick back by the fire, and be prepared for a story that may make your teeth chatter just a bit—and if it does, believe me, it won't be from the cold.

1. Sunlight Camp

· ·

Since I live in Colorado, I decided I would try and hit some of the Bigfoot hotspots in my home state first, even though I was anxious to get up into Montana, one of my favorite places, and also where I had some unfinished business.

So, wherever I went on my Bigfoot expedition, I knew I would end up in Montana eventually—but to start out, I wanted to visit some nearby hotspots in Colorado.

I'd always been interested in the Flattop Mountains in the west-central part of the state, as a number of interesting stories have come from there, both from my fishing clients as well as from numerous others.

The Flattops would be my first destination, I decided. It was close enough to home that I could retreat if I found I'd forgotten something (and as you can see, I was making up excuses for escape even at the very beginning of the whole escapade).

As an aside, if you've read my book, "The Bigfoot Runes," you'll already be familiar with that area, especially Coffeepot Springs, the location of the Rune Cave. Did I go looking there? No, even though I knew the general area it was in, I didn't, out of respect for Packy, who told me the story. That's his story, not mine, and I didn't want to intrude on any of that. Or maybe I was too nervous, to be honest.

Anyway, I studied my topo maps of the Flattops, packed up my old pickup with my tent and camping gear, bought a few groceries, said goodbye to Sarah (wondering if I'd ever see her again, though she didn't seem too worried), and headed south.

As you'll soon see, this beginning of my month-long so-called Bigfoot "expedition" was filled with anticipation, excitement, and more than just a little anxiety.

The Flattops weren't all that far, just a few hours away, and I was soon at the road that climbed up onto their western flanks, near Meeker, Colorado, clear on the other side of the range from Coffeepot Springs.

The road to the little town of Buford went about as deep in the Flattops as one could get on a paved road, which was pretty deep, and all I would have to do is find a side road and follow it for a ways to get into fairly rugged country. Getting way back in should be pretty easy, I thought. But already my plans were being thwarted.

What I had hoped would be a perfect Colorado bluebird day was not to be—the summer monsoons had started a little early. Mists floated around, giving the place a mysterious feel and heightening a sense of dread I was beginning to feel for no discernible reason.

And the higher I got, the wetter things became, with signs of small flash-floods, places where mud and rocks had been washed across the road. I was soon to find that, in spite of the weather and forecast being fairly good for that part of the state, it was actually starting to really get hit. I'd checked the weather, but all it had said was scattered rain showers, so someone at the weather service had been overly optimistic, I guess.

Finally, I made it up to Buford, where the mists had turned into a heavy drizzle. After seeing a red fox run across the road, drenched, its tail between its legs, I decided to turn back. No point camping in the pouring rain—I'd feel like that poor fox—and I already felt like I was starting out with my tail between my legs, so to say, anyway.

After some thought, I decided I would keep going south and reconnoiter. I had a good friend over in Rifle, Colorado, which wasn't too far. I would stop by his place and see if he was free and wanted to go camping, and maybe wait out the weather there at his house for a bit. And as you can see, I was already showing a reluctance to continue, a feeling that haunted me for almost the entire expedition.

Anyway, I was slowly working my way up to (or maybe out of) the concept of camping alone, even though I'd done it for years and was used to being alone out in the backcountry. But something was different now—there was something about chasing after Bigfoot that gave a whole new feeling to the enterprise.

My friend, Mark, was home, and I felt a sense of real homeyness when he invited me inside his little house. I normally would never consider town life to be desirable, as I like wide open spaces without any people, but it felt different now, for some reason. It felt comforting.

And I knew what that reason was—I was starting to feel really insecure about this new mission. I was already missing Sarah, and I hadn't been gone more than a half-day! I was used to being apart from her, out with my clients by some remote river, but now I wanted to be with her. This feeling would also continue through my trip and sometimes even take on an almost desperate sense.

But don't give up on me yet—there's more to this adventure than my wanting to end it, as you'll soon see, even though the thought was on my mind the entire month I was gone.

So, at Mark's, I sank down in his old couch, the same one I'd slept on numerous times back when he lived in Steamboat and worked at the ski area there, back before Sarah and I had been married.

The fact that it still had the same missing springs felt comforting, for some reason. I just wanted to kick my feet up and take a nap and forget this crazy project I'd signed myself up for.

Completely unlike me, I ended up staying there for two days, eating Mark's groceries and crashing on his couch. This was something I would normally never do. His cupboards were filled with junk food, and it tasted really good—sugar and fats.

Sarah would have been appalled, but I thoroughly enjoyed my regression into my pre-responsibility era, back to the days when I was in college studying wildlife biology, which is where I'd met Mark—in fact, we'd been college roommates.

So, through all this, Mark was at his job with UPS while I hung around his house all day, just vegging and playing ball with his cute little Corgi, Ginger, delaying the inevitable. I would soon need to get on with it or give up on it. I wasn't sure which choice suited me best, but I was beginning to think it was the "give up on it" one.

Finally, the weather broke, and Mark and I headed out. He had somehow managed to get a week off and said he'd go camping with me, as long as I provided the food, since I'd practically wiped him out. At that point, I would've paid him good money to go with me, so buying some extra food was of no concern.

And of course the weather pattern called for more rain. We decided to take our chances and go anyway, heading up into the forest above the ski area near Glenwood Springs, a thriving tourist town just down the road from Mark's house.

He knew a nice little camp spot in a good central location, and neither of us was eager to go get stuck, so it seemed like a good choice.

It wasn't too far as the crow flies from where one of my clients had been followed by a Bigfoot, so even though it wasn't what I called a Bigfoot hotspot, who knows, maybe we'd see something. The Flattops would have to wait for another day.

We drove through the busy tourist town of Glenwood Springs, turning and crossing a bridge over the scenic Roaring Fork River.

I had an almost uncontrollable urge to stop and go fly-fishing, as that particular river has some of the best Blue Ribbon waters in Colorado, which means darn big trout. I felt a sense of poignancy, like I might never get to go fishing again.

A lush narrow valley followed pristine Four Mile Creek as we climbed up and up towards Ski Sunlight, the local ski area, and it didn't take long to get to the camp spot that Mark had mentioned, about 10 miles from town.

The spot was on the remnant of an old road that ran into a long abandoned logging camp, though the road was now blocked by huge rocks, presumably bulldozed into place by the old D9 Allis Chalmers Caterpillar that set nearby, rusted and silent since what appeared to be the 1960s.

About 40 feet above the camp spot ran the county road we'd come in on, and several hundred feet below was a wide area where a beaver dam slowed the creek down, creating a lush bog that was now home to moose, recently introduced to the area. I wasn't real crazy about the thought of being near moose, as they can be dangerous.

High above, I could see the top of Sunlight Peak, a 10,574-foot mountain where several radio and microwave towers stretched to the sky, red lights flashing on and off as a warning to aircraft.

After being there awhile, I named this spot Sunlight Camp because it set about 700 feet below the top of the peak. It was an ironic name, since we seldom saw the sun while we were there. The camp was high enough to make for some cold nights, and I wished for a big warm coat like a Bigfoot wears—but without a Bigfoot in it.

The camp itself was surrounded by mature aspen trees, some over a foot in diameter, and some around 30 feet tall, if not taller. A beautiful understory of currents, skunkbush, wild rose, ferns, and tons of wildflowers spoke of a place that received lots of rain, and we were to confirm this during our stay, as the week or so we spent there it rained five out of the seven days. By the time we left, the road had turned into a bog, and it was touch and go to not get stuck.

But, in spite of the rain, it was a beautiful place, with very few mosquitoes and a few flies that came out the few times it stopped raining.

We set up our tents just as fog moved in below us, followed by heavy rain and wind bending the trees, along with lightning and thunder. The monsoons seemed determined to get the better of us.

But as Mark and I sat in my tent for awhile, talking a bit, the rain suddenly stopped. I went out and managed to collect enough semi-dry firewood to get a small fire going.

And now, after making a cup of hot chocolate, I began to feel a bit better about this expedition. I wondered why I'd felt so uncertain earlier. Now, the forest felt benign. It seemed like I was slowly regaining my old self, now that I was back in the outdoors—and I knew that having someone with me was also helping.

Almost dark, I could see a damp mist coming along the valley below us. We were sitting by what had quickly become a wet and sputtering campfire, contemplating going to bed, when we both jumped at what sounded like a large rock being thumped onto the ground in the distance.

I strained to see through the falling dusk, as I immediately thought of Bigfoot. Sure enough, we heard it again— whoo-thump. Mark and I looked at each other in the dark, then he said, simply, "Thunder. Way over towards Basalt Mountain."

I had no idea why, but the feeling of uncertainty had returned, and it stuck with me the entire time we were there, which we spent mostly sitting around a campfire eating and talking, or running into town, just for something to do. We had planned to go hiking on a nearby trail, but the weather was damp and chilly, and we seemed to have lost any and all ambition.

And at night, I would lie in my tent and wonder if there were Bigfoot nearby. My plan to just hang out and wait for them to come visit me seemed seriously flawed. Why would they? Surely they had seen their fill of humans, the way we seemed to encroach everywhere and on everything.

I did have one scare while there—I was moving my metal camp table and boom! I heard and saw lighting at the same time. I thought for a moment I was dead, then it dawned on me that if I'd been struck, I wouldn't have time to think about it.

Finally, it was our last morning there, and I got up at dawn, just as the rain stopped. I broke camp, wishing it had been better weather, throwing my wet soggy tent into the back of my pickup. Hopefully I could find a dryer clime, as I would have to set the tent up later to dry out, or it would mold.

Listening to my little hand-cranked weather radio, waiting for Mark to get up, it seemed that most of Western Colorado had flash flood warnings. Everywhere I had planned to go on my expedition was under a flood warning.

It had rained long enough that by now everything was fully saturated, and they were also predicting mudflows, especially on the burn scars from some recent fires. I wondered how my Bigfoot friends were doing, assuming they were even out there. I was relieved that we hadn't had any visits.

Finally, around 8 a.m., Mark got up, and I got out my little cook stove and put water on to boil for coffee. We sat in our camp chairs, drinking coffee and talking, not in a hurry to leave, Ginger at Mark's feet.

Suddenly, we heard a sound coming from the deep valley below us. We listened for awhile, then Mark said, "There's someone down there."

I replied, "Why would someone be down in that bog in the fog?"

"I don't know. Maybe it's a hiker."

"More like a wader—or swimmer."

Ginger had been unusually quiet and subdued since we'd first got there, but we figured it was the weather. Mark had remarked on it the day before, worried that the little dog might not be feeling well. She kept wanting to be in his tent all the time, curled up on his sleeping bag. She now sat up, perking her ears intently in the direction of the noise.

It's hard to describe, but it sounded almost like a person, except it was a bit too high pitched and loud. It came again:

"Hey! Hey!"

We sat, silent.

"Hey, you, you!"

It wasn't quite like a human would say it, but the words were close, though more high-pitched and ethereal, if one can imagine an ethereal sound.

It was now mid-morning, but the thick clouds made it feel almost timeless. Everything seemed quiet and ominous.

For some reason, I suddenly lost all fear and had the urge to creep through the thick aspens for a peek down the hill, but the terrain was too steep and thick with understory, as well as slippery. Later, I wondered if something had been subconsciously influencing me, something like my own original desire to see a Bigfoot, the desire that seemed to have been overcome by my fears.

I sneezed, and the sound stopped. Was it a coincidence, or could whatever it was hear me from clear down in the valley?

We sat there, and soon the yells came again. Whatever it was, it seemed to be stationary. It was just yelling, not like anything in the Bigfoot encounters I'd heard about, where the sound is deep and thick and carries for miles.

This almost seemed friendly—loud enough to carry up the valley to where we sat, but not something one would hear for more than a half-mile or so. We could now hear the raucous sound of magpies coming from the same area.

Mark got up, took down his tent, and threw it into the back of my pickup. I turned on my weather radio again, which said the temperature on Sunlight Peak was now 48 degrees. Apparently there was a weather station up there with the microwave towers.

As the fog continued drifting through the valley, we continued listening. The sound continued off and on for an hour, coming from the same place below us.

Mark was now back in his chair, looking a bit nervous.

He finally asked, "Aren't you worried about what that might be?"

"Maybe it's a bird," I replied calmly.

"A pretty big bird."

"Loon cries carry for miles."

"You think that's a loon?"

"Not in this part of Colorado."

"What is it?"

"Your guess is as good as mine."

We were going in circles, getting nowhere.

"Rusty, how about what we came here for? You think it somehow knows?"

"No. If it *is* a Bigfoot, it's a coincidence. It wouldn't know we were here looking for it. I don't think so, anyway."

I didn't sound very convincing.

"What should we do?"

"Exactly what we're doing. Maybe have some more coffee."

"You're a funny guy. Aren't you nervous?"

"Not really. If it is a Bigfoot, it would be cool if it would come on up. Maybe have a cup of coffee with us."

I was joking around to hide my true feelings, for even though it was broad daylight, I was torn between staying and going. After all, this was my reason for this trip—to try to prove the existence of Bigfoot, and yet my instincts were telling me to get going.

Now Ginger was on high alert, eyes staring into the wet aspen forest and ears standing straight up. We hadn't heard the yelling for a few minutes. Ginger began to growl, then went to my truck, wanting in badly, standing on her rear legs with her front feet up against the door.

Mark stood, folded his camp chair and threw it into the back of my truck, then lifted Ginger into the front, her little legs too short for her to jump in.

I followed suit, throwing my chair into the back, then jumped into the pickup cab. We were now all in the truck, but I hadn't yet started it.

I said, "Let's sit here a minute and see what happens."

"I think we should go," Mark replied nervously.

It was now starting to sprinkle. I turned on the pickup and slowly drove it down the long muddy lane, hoping I didn't get stuck. Had all the rains brought whatever was yelling at us down from the higher territories? Part of me still wanted to stay, but not badly enough to argue with Mark.

Soon on the county road and headed back to town, we passed Ski Sunlight, and the rain stopped, the sun breaking through the dark clouds. I felt a sense of relief, and I could tell Mark did, too.

"I think I'm going to reconsider this camping thing," he finally said solemnly.

I said nothing, though I was thinking the same thing. The whole time we were there, my intuition said we shouldn't be. But why? Our camp was near a traveled road, a road that people from town came up to hike or take their dogs out, not some pristine wilderness way in the outback.

Later, I recalled the couple of times, when the breeze was still, that we could hear the clacking of rocks, as if some large animal was walking through them—elk, maybe?

And once, we had heard something really strange—it sounded like something gnawing on a bone, something back in the forest across the road above us. It was truly odd.

Sunlight Camp had definitely been a Bigfooty place, but was it really? Other than the strange gnawing sound and the yelling, if one weren't thinking of Bigfoot, nothing would seem out of the ordinary—they were just sounds of the forest.

Yet how could we explain the yelling?

I had no answers, and I knew I should go back to Sunlight Camp again sometime, though I never did.

2. The Big Blue

· ·

My good friend, Jay, once described in terrifying detail his experience while hiking in the Big Blue of southern Colorado (now called the Uncompahgre Wilderness).

He was sleeping in his tent when something had stomped around it through the entire night and at one point even pulled the tent up a bit off the ground. Whatever it was, it had to have hands to do that.

And so, I had included the Big Blue on my itinerary as a Bigfoot hotspot. I'd camped in this beautiful section of Colorado's San Juan Mountains, but had never backpacked there, like Jay often did.

After taking Mark home and staying at his place yet another day, I gave Jay a call, asking if he wanted to go into the Big Blue for a few days. We would drive up the long rough road into the East Fork of the Cimarron River and camp, maybe doing a day hike or two up into the wilderness area with its stunning rugged mountains.

He was eager to go, and yup, that sounded like Jay to me. He never turned down a chance to get into the back-

country, even if it meant dodging work or any other re-
sponsibilities he might have. Like me, he lived to be outdoors. And like me, he was a big fan of Bigfoot.

So, I drove the 180 miles or so and met Jay in Montrose.
He was a native of the area and had spent years hiking
the San Juan Mountains and had also had another Bigfoot
encounter there. He'd been in his tent when several of the
large creatures walked silently by in the moonlight, casting
huge shadows.

Long before I met and married Sarah, Jay and I had
spent many nights camping together, scareing each other
with Bigfoot stories, never dreaming we'd both have encounters or near-encounters. Jay and I had been friends
since meeting at a mutual friend's house. He was a wildlife
biologist by training, just as I was, but he'd made a career
of it, while I had instead become a fishing guide.

So, we left Montrose and were soon driving up the
East Fork of the Cimarron River into the Cimarron Range,
a subrange of the San Juans, where we spent the night
camped in a meadow by my pickup. The next morning, we
gathered our day gear and hiked a popular trail that led
deep into the Big Blue Wilderness.

We had decided to hike in five or six miles, hoping to
get up into the basin under Wetterhorn Peak, have lunch,
then turn around and be out by dark. It would be a long
day. This whole area seemed like a good place for Bigfoot,
and we'd both heard a number of stories.

It was a long trudge with quite a bit of altitude gain, and
I can't say fly-fishing is one of the more aerobic sports, so
the hike took its toll on me. Jay was in much better shape,

as he was better acclimated to the altitude. I was glad I'd spent some time up at Sunlight Camp, or I might've been in even worse shape.

We finally came to a high alpine meadow, where I collapsed, leaning against an old gnarly pine tree. Across the valley stood the sharp-edged Wetterhorn Peak, one of Colorado's more dramatic Fourteeners at 14,015 feet, with a sheer face on one side. Our topo map said we were at 11,000 feet, and I sure could feel it.

We pulled out our sandwiches and gorp and sat and ate, silent. I was too exhausted to want to talk much, mostly feeling a lack of oxygen. After eating, I wanted to take a nap, which is common in such scenarios. Lack of oxygen, or hypoxia, can make you feel like sleeping—and I was soon sawing logs.

Hypoxia can also make you feel anxious, which is possibly why, when I awoke, I felt that sense of dread that had been plaguing me on and off all along, only now it was much stronger.

Jay was gone.

His pack was still where he'd left it, but there was no sign where he was off to. I stood and called out, but there was no reply. Where had he gone, and why?

I felt more and more anxious and wanted to run away. I needed to get down to a lower altitude where I could breathe better. And to make things worse, misty clouds were now closing in around the top of Wetterhorn Peak. It looked like the monsoons were catching up to us yet again. It was time to go.

I put my pack on and picked up Jay's and zipped it up. I walked a bit out into the clearing, where I could see out better, and began yelling again.

"Jay! Jay! Where are you? Jay!"

I now began to think of Winston Branko Churchill, a hiker who'd gone missing in this area a few years back. He was a savvy outdoorsman and had spent two months hiking the Colorado Trail before veering off into the Big Blue, where he'd lost contact with the friends who had been resupplying him via care packages. A search had turned up nothing, and sadly, he'd been found dead the next spring, emaciated and frozen, right outside a well-stocked cabin.

Why had Churchill gone missing? Some thought it was through choice, as he was estranged from civilization and searching for a new life. This had nothing to do with Bigfoot, as far as I knew, but I couldn't help but think of him, now that Jay was apparently missing.

My anxiety was increasing by the minute, and it was all I could do to stay put and not run madly back down the trail. I recognized mentally that what was happening was from a lack of oxygen, but I couldn't help it, I wanted to get out right then and there.

"Jay! Jay!"

My voice sounded odd to me, all panicky.

Suddenly, Jay was next to me. He'd slipped out of the forest behind me, startling me.

"What's up, man?" He sounded a bit puzzled.

"I was wondering where you'd gone to," I answered lamely, relieved.

"I just hiked over to look at that outcrop over there while you were sleeping. You OK?" Jay looked concerned.

"I need to get out of here. I'm feeling a bit anxious. It's the thin air."

Jay grabbed his pack, and we were soon hiking back down the trail at a much faster clip than we'd come up. I was starting to feel better, the movement making the blood flow, or maybe it was from our dropping in elevation.

Jay was ahead of me, and he suddenly stopped, holding up his hand to be quiet. We stood there on the trail, and what we heard made my blood turn cold, as they say.

Below us, across the other side of the narrow East Fork of the Cimarron, came a sound unlike anything I'd ever heard before or since. It sounded like a man dying—there was no other way to describe it. It was truly horrible. It was a combination of screaming and gurgling. It put the hackles up on my neck.

I turned to Jay and his face held the same look I'm sure mine held—one of shock. We both were thinking someone was being killed down there, right below us.

I whispered, "What should we do?"

As we stood there, listening, it finally dawned on me that there was something a bit off about the sound. Just like the yelling I'd heard at Sunlight Camp, this initially sounded human, but yet had an odd inhuman quality to it.

Jay whispered back, "Run like hell!"

Neither of us were cowards, and we'd both had plenty of times when we'd stopped to help someone in need, even if it were just minor things like helping with a flat tire or getting someone unstuck. We weren't the types to not help out when needed, but the longer we listened, the more we believed this wasn't someone in need at all. It felt like a ruse.

We took off running and running, and it actually felt good to stretch out and get the heck out of there. After a half-mile or so, my lungs were aching, and I had to stop. I leaned against a tree, breathing so hard I couldn't talk. I half expected to hear something coming along the trail behind us, but all was quiet.

After resting a bit, we continued hiking at a good pace, and it wasn't long before we were back at my pickup. We didn't stop, but just jumped in and took off down the road.

A couple of hours later, we were back at Jay's house. He invited me in, and we talked for awhile about everything, but neither of us had any idea of what had just happened.

As we sat there, we discussed whether or not we'd been remiss by running away. Could it have been a mountain lion? They were good screamers and had scared many braver than us. And what if it had really been someone needing help? We both knew better, but Jay decided to call the sheriff anyway.

After explaining what had happened, he hung up with a chagrined look on his face.

"He told me they'd keep an eye out, but I don't think he took it very seriously," Jay reported.

I hung out at Jay's a little longer, then decided it was time to leave. I needed to keep my momentum going or I knew I'd have a repeat of what had happened at Mark's—hanging out way too long, missing Sarah, and building up even more trepidation, which would be even easier to do after all this. I had to keep moving.

I was soon on the highway, heading south, even though it was late. I would spend the night sleeping in the back of my truck somewhere along the road.

This was only my second week out and I'd already found more possible Bigfootery than I'd hoped for. Were these creatures really as rare as some think, or did they somehow recognize I was searching for them? Or had the sounds been Bigfoot at all?

I recalled one of my clients who'd had a scary encounter, and who had said it's not a good idea to go searching for them. But there I'd been, in the thick of a vast wilderness, kind of searching, in a way, or chasing after Bigfoot, I called it.

I knew Bigfoot could easily exist in Colorado, even though some say the species is confined to the Pacific Northwest. There was plenty of wildness in just the Big Blue alone where Bigfoot could easily wander without being bothered. And what of the vast forests of Canada, not to mention the thick forests of places like Minnesota and even the Appalachians? It shouldn't be hard to see that Bigfoot has plenty of possible habitat. Check out Google Earth if you don't believe me.

And so, there in Colorado's Big Blue was more possible evidence for Bigfoot's existence, and yet, even though I was convinced, I still had nothing convincing I could show a skeptic. Maybe that's the essence of the mystery—belief. But science requires more than belief, and I felt that my search for real evidence had to continue.

I'd only been at my second spot, and it felt like I'd again fled, just like I had at the first, Sunlight Peak, though this time I was actually running. I had to admit to being un-comfortable—even scared—which went against my feel-ings about these great creatures. Sure, I'd heard plenty of stories about how dangerous they could be, but I somehow figured those had been rogues, not the norm.

Just as I tend to give my fellow humans the benefit of the doubt upon first meeting, I was sure most Bigfoot had no desire to harm humans. And sure, there are sto-ries about people going missing in the wilds, but I really believe that most cases are due to inexperience and poor judgement, not wild animals, especially not Bigfoot.

My only fears in the wilds (and I'd spent much of my life out there alone) were of my own stupidity, like the near-lightning strike at Sunlight Camp where I should've been sitting in my truck, not moving gear around.

So, it was strike two out of two so far. Would I always be running away when things got sketchy, always fleeing?

After thinking about it, I decided Jay's admonishment to "run like hell" had just fed into all my other fears. I needed to start going out by myself if I wanted more control over such situations, for even if I were afraid, then I alone could make the decision of whether or not to continue.

As I drove along, I decided that my next destination would be the home of the Howler, and I would go alone. The thought gave me a chill, but also a feeling of elation. Perhaps there I would find what I was searching for.

I was soon to find that I had less mettle alone than I'd thought I would have—much less.

3. The Howler

Colorado's southern San Juan Mountains contain some of the most rugged wilderness on the planet. Even short distances become daunting when in the San Juans—it's a land of volcanic verticality, high mountain cirques, avalanches, raging creeks, and well, there has to also be Bigfoot.

My friend Jack had sent me an amazing photo of Bigfoot prints he'd taken in the southern San Juans, where some wildlife biologists believe grizzly bears may still live. Jack hadn't even believed in Bigfoot before that, but he said seeing the prints way out there, backpacking alone, gave him the creeps.

There was no way it could've been a hoax—he was alone, miles out on foot in some of the most rugged country in the U.S., and he hadn't seen a soul for over a week. The prints were along a small creek that wasn't anywhere near a trail.

This wild region was once home to grizzly bears, the last which was killed in the 1970s. Rumor has it that there are more there, and numerous wildlife biologists have spent months in the deep wilds looking for them, finding nothing.

But biologists say this region is one of the best habitats in Colorado for species dependent on areas largely untrod by humans, such as the grizzly and wolverine. Yet it seems the search for Bigfoot yields even less evidence than that for the grizz—unless you count the eerie recordings of what's become known as the Howler.

Before this trip, I was typically more afraid of grizzly and moose than of Bigfoot. People often don't realize that moose can easily kill a human—and sometimes do. Since moose have recently been reintroduced to Colorado, I have a heightened awareness when out hiking and fishing in their territory.

But one thing that's scared me even more than moose and bears is the Howler. That name is used to describe a Bigfoot that haunts the San Juan River in northern New Mexico, but it's also the name given to a creature deep in Colorado's southern San Juans that's been recorded several times by various people.

I'll never forget the call from my friend, Sammy. He'd been backpacking in the region near Vallecito Lake, near Durango, doing research on some kind of alpine wood-pecker for his Master's thesis in biology.

He was carrying some sophisticated recording equip-ment and was able to record the Howler, though he didn't plan to, as he'd never even heard of it before the night it came into his camp.

Sammy woke to something shuffling around near his tent, and he instinctively turned on his recorder, being a wildlife biologist in research mode. What he recorded left him lying motionless through the entire night, frozen in fear, waiting only for the morning light so he could pack up and get out.

When I heard the recording, I felt like I was listening to something from long ago, some primal creature that had long been gone, probably exterminated by humans so they could sleep at night. Of course, I do believe early humans may have killed an occasional Bigfoot, but I believe the species still exists, and the Howler proves it to anyone who has felt that sense of fear mixed with wonder that such creatures inspire.

I can't imagine what it must have been like to live with the huge megafauna our Pleistocene ancestors did—I can't imagine it until I hear something like the Howler, that is.

When I heard Sammy's recording, I was stunned. The creature apparently messed around in his camp a bit, then wandered back out into the nearby forest, where it began howling. Even though Sammy said he heard it crashing through the brush for some time before it stopped, it still sounded like it was right outside his tent, that's how loud it was.

Describing the sound isn't easy, but it had an incredible husky sound, and it must have had big lungs, as each howl went on for a good 20 seconds or more. It started out with a low "ahh," which then became a higher-pitched "ooo" that went on and on.

Sammy said he at first thought maybe he was listening to a wolf that had strayed down from Montana or Wyoming, but the intensity and loudness of the howl just didn't fit that theory. And when the howl turned into a sort of chatter sound, he knew it was no wolf.

Available on the internet, the writings of hunter Keith Foster present a number of compelling Bigfoot accounts in this area of the San Juan Mountains. But anyway, back to my story, as I'm getting sidetracked.

After spending the night wrapped up in my sleeping bag in the back of my truck in the back parking lot of a small outdoors store in the little town of Ridgway, I drove on down to the town of Durango in the southern San Juans.

Sammy had drawn me a map of where he'd been, but I had no intentions of backpacking deep into the timber like he had. I would follow my existing modus operandi and car camp.

I restocked on fresh groceries at Durango, then headed up the road to Vallecito Lake. Once up there, I would follow the old road that had been Sammy's jump-off place, then tent camp there by my pickup in a small meadow Sammy had told me about. That was as deep in the wilderness as I intended to go.

The feeling of impending doom still hung over me like a black cloud, especially since I'd decided that if I were going to go into the wilds alone, I might as well go into the area that contained the particular Bigfoot that I knew had the potential to scare me to death. Might as well do it right.

In retrospect, there was only one thing I wish I'd done differently. After having had two possible encounters so far, both which were not visual but were instead audible, you'd think it would have dawned on me to buy a recording device of some kind.

The thought did cross my mind, but I was running pretty tight on the money front and already had a good camera, so I figured—well, I don't know what I figured. Going in search of an elusive creature and hoping to document it for science or whatever and not having the right tools just doesn't make any sense to me now. But at the time, I just didn't have the money.

So, I made it to the spot on Sammy's map and got out and stretched, looking around. It was a beautiful meadow, surrounded by a mix of aspens and pine, with tall grasses and a small creek running through the far edge. It being early August, there were lots of wildflowers in bloom.

As I stood there, soaking in the beauty of the mountains, I began to wish I had a dog. Why didn't I have a dog? I loved animals, and dogs always took to me. Mark's dog Ginger had been great company, and her doggie senses had made me feel more comfortable. I missed her putting her paw on my arm so I would pet her.

I'd thought before of getting a dog, but being gone so much as a guide kind of put a crimp in the idea, making it seem impractical. But as I stood there, I decided I would get a dog. It could go fishing and camping with me, and most of my fishing clients seemed to be dog lovers, so what was the problem?

I got out my little camp stove and warmed up a can of Spaghetti-O's, thinking of Sarah—she would be appalled to see what I was eating. But for some reason, it tasted good, along with a piece of flatbread I'd bought at the store. I washed it all down with water, though I would've preferred a good can of brew at that point. I hadn't bought any beer, trying to be frugal.

I sat in my camp chair, watching a fiery sunset, then decided to just sleep on the ground on my pad rather than go to the trouble of setting up my little tent. That way I could star gaze as I went to sleep.

These high mountains don't have much in way of biting bugs or things that bother you in the night—except mosquitos, which can be horrendous at certain times but which didn't seem to be a problem when I was there. The only other thing that can bite you are predators, but most of these are afraid of humans. I wanted to sleep out where I wouldn't miss anything. I guess I'd decided to face my fears, as they say.

I now sat very still on a log, trying to take in the feeling of this wild and untouched place. After the sun had set, I began to feel a bit uncertain, that feeling I'm sure many have felt when the dusk makes everything mysterious, our human eyes not all that adapted to the dark.

As I sat there, I thought I heard monkey chatter, but then realized it was ravens. How odd for them to sound like monkeys, I thought, aware that my mind was prepped for Bigfoot.

Ravens are great imitators and can even be taught words when in captivity, and I later wondered if they'd heard Bigfoot chatter and had learned to imitate it. This of course occurred to me some time afterwords, or I would've been in an even more heightened frame of mind, which would have been hard to do.

As the darkness deepened, I finally climbed into my sleeping bag and watched the night sky open up. You can't imagine what the stars look like at an altitude around 10,000 feet and in that clear atmosphere—they actually seem to be hanging up there in layers, they're so thick.

Why was I so afraid of the Howler? The sounds it had made on Sammy's recording were indeed strange, but I'd heard other purported Bigfoot recordings without them having that effect on me. Maybe it was because it was closer to my home territory, I thought. But in truth, it really wasn't all that close, as my home in northern Colorado was now several hundred miles away.

The Howler had almost sounded like a wolf to me. I again thought of what it must have been like 10,000 years ago during the Pleistocene. Maybe the recording was touching on some primal fear from way back when our ancestors feared the great Pleistocene predators, the dire wolves and cave bears and sabertooth tigers.

I was glad I at least didn't have to worry about such things, like a giant mastodon stepping on me in the night.

I lay there in the darkness, straining to hear any strange noises, when I thought I heard something yelling far away in the distance. It sounded like it was miles away, like maybe a bull bellowing—a long drawn-out low sound.

As I lay there, my heart beating fast, I decided I had to get a grip on my fears. It seemed like I'd been afraid of my own shadow ever since I'd been at Sunlight Peak.

I just couldn't figure it out. Here I was, in one of the most beautiful places on Earth, and my heart was beating so hard I couldn't hear the silence. It wasn't at all like me, as I spend most of my time in remote places fly-fishing. I've always felt comfortable in the wilds.

I climbed out of my sleeping bag and pulled my little camp stove from my pickup. I would have some peppermint tea—that would help me sleep.

As I sat and drank the hot tea, all was quiet—there were no more noises from the forest, not a peep. All I could see was the outline of the treetops against the starriest sky I'd ever seen.

Now, I suddenly wanted a fire. I turned on my headlamp and walked around a bit, but there was no wood around. I knew I'd have to venture into the woods to find any, so I let it go. It would be a fireless night.

I've never been much for fires when alone, though I love sitting around them with others. There's something about a fire that makes me feel vulnerable—I can't see into the darkness as well, and the fire makes me more visible to anything out there—a fire tells the entire world where you are.

But that night, I badly wanted a fire. It seemed like a good defense—but against what? As far as I knew, there was nothing out there.

Finally, I pulled my pad and sleeping bag right up next to the pickup door so all I would have to do is stand up and get in, if something happened. I was still feeling spooked.

I also pulled my camp chair over against the pickup, then sat down, leaning back in the dark. Would the Howler make an appearance? Part of me wanted to hear it for myself, but a bigger part of me wanted it to stay far far away. I'd felt the same over in the Big Blue and up at Sunlight Peak. Some Bigfoot hunter I was turning out to be.

But I wasn't really hunting Bigfoot, was I? It seemed to me I was instead putting myself into situations where they could hunt me. Chasing after Bigfoot was a misnomer—I was simply hoping to have an encounter.

I shivered, then suddenly froze. There was something over on the edge of the meadow—I could barely make out a figure darker than the grasses. It must have seen me, as it appeared to also freeze in place. It wasn't large, about the size of a small cougar. I strained to see it better, but it was now gone. Probably just a coyote.

I laughed at myself—afraid of a coyote. It was so dark that I couldn't even see my truck, which was right next to me. And still no Howler. I wondered if I shouldn't try to call it in by woodknocking or yelling.

But then, just like before, I suddenly started missing Sarah, missing our little trailer just out of town, missing the warmth of civilization. I felt on the edge like I'd never felt before.

What was I doing out here? Why in the world would I want to try and call the Howler in? My answers seemed illogical and silly. Chasing after Bigfoot, the most elusive creature in North America. What a futile endeavor. I must be nuts.

I decided I was making myself a basket case, and I should either pack everything up, admit defeat, and go home, or else go to bed. I opted for the latter, crawling down into my bag.

Finally managing to relax a bit, I started humming Red River Valley, which my mom used to sing to me when I was a little kid, but it felt like I was making too much noise, so I lapsed into silence.

As I lay there, I suddenly heard something coming from the forest on two feet, something really heavy, and I swore I could hear ravens chattering like monkeys—or was it my imagination? Why would ravens be up that time of night? They roost at night, don't they?

Maybe it was some cattle coming to graze in the meadow. But the walking sound and the ravens or whatever it was stopped as quickly as it had begun.

I knew I should get up and get into my truck, but I suddenly felt very tired, very weary. All the stress had taken its toll on me. The last thing I remembered was pulling my down bag up over my ears.

When I woke, it was almost dawn, and I had the feeling something woke me. I pulled myself from my bag and stood up. The stars were even thicker than before, as if someone had painted yet another layer of stars over the existing layers while I slept.

I took a leak behind the truck, then crawled back into my bag, still tired. But as I started to drift back off, something told me to get up—something suddenly felt very wrong.

I felt like someone must feel when suffering from hypothermia—you want nothing more than to sleep, but in the back of your mind you know you have to get up or you'll die.

I crawled back out of my bag, tossed it and my camp chair and pad into the truck, jumped into the cab, and locked the doors.

Now I thought I could see something over at the edge of the woods, at the same place the coyote had been, but I wasn't really sure. But try as I might, I couldn't keep my eyes open. I drifted back to sleep, head leaning on the window.

When I again awoke, the sun was beating down, making my head sweat against the glass. My neck was stiff, and I felt like I should leave immediately. Even though it was now broad daylight, I still felt that something was wrong.

I got out and walked around a bit. I looked for tracks, but found none, and there was really no reason to feel so uncertain, but I just couldn't help it.

It was then that I thought I could again hear monkey chatter—it must be those darn ravens, I thought—until suddenly the tenor of the calls changed and became much lower.

I started my truck and left, not looking back.

Once back in Durango, I stopped at a little diner and got breakfast, drinking lots of coffee, even though it tasted bitter and boiled. I was very happy to be surrounded by people. I called Sarah, but she didn't answer, and I knew she was busy at work.

As I headed on down the road, I had plenty of time to think, and I berated myself again for my fears.

Back on the open highway, making good time, I knew it was time to leave Colorado. There were a number of Bigfoot hotspots I hadn't visited there, but I wanted to work my way up to Montana. I felt relieved, to be honest, at finally getting out of the San Juans and charting a new course.

The mountains were soon far behind, a low rise of jagged peaks in my rear-view mirror. I crossed into Utah, turned north, and drove on. It was good to be in the desert, and I stopped in the tourist town of Moab and resupplied at the grocery store there, even getting myself an espresso.

As evening came, I found myself on a side road in the desert near Green River, Utah. I could see for miles, and there wasn't a tree in sight, and it felt good. No Bigfoot here. I set up camp and relaxed for once, unafraid, enjoying the balmy temperatures.

Then, as I relaxed, a distant memory came to me, haunting me. Was it real or a dream? Could I have really heard the Howler at dawn back near Vallecito Lake? Was that what had awakened me?

I shivered in the warm desert air.

4. Desert Danger

· ·

Possibly one of the strangest things that has ever happened to me occurred next—not in a deep twilight-lit forest, as one would expect when Bigfooting, but instead out in the barren desert.

I've always loved the wide open vistas and stunning sunsets of the deserts of the American Southwest, and If I didn't make my living as a fishing guide, I would probably turn into a desert rat. And after camping in the Colorado monsoons, being in the dry Utah desert was a treat. I could finally dry out all my gear.

As far as what happened next, all I can say is I was again missing Sarah, so instead of using my head for thinking and being aware of my surroundings, I was using it to feel sorry for myself.

I felt that my Bigfoot chasing had been a disaster so far, primarily because of my unfettered fears. Now that I had some time to devote to my passion for Bigfoot, I was turning into a bundle of nerves. So, regarding what happened next, I should've paid more attention but didn't. It was that simple.

I set up my tent and camp chair, feeling comfortable and safe in the wide openness of the desert. The only potential dangers here are snakes and scorpions, and these will leave you alone if you give them the same regard.

I'd camped in this same desert with Sarah, and she'd given me a geology lesson—this particular stretch of badlands was all Mancos shale, laid down when the region was under water millions of years ago. The Mancos looks like the surface of the moon might look—shades of whites and grays. And it's almost as barren—though it's actually somewhat fertile soil, it has almost no plant life from a lack of water.

There's nothing out here—no bears or mountain lions (or so I thought), and where I was camped was too dry even for snakes, as the rodents were few and far between, and snakes eat rodents as their primary meal. There were a few more red ants around than I cared for, but I decoyed them with some cracker crumbs on the other side of my camp so they'd leave me alone, which they did.

It was soon sunset, and I was intently watching the sun go down over the big wide horizon, watching for the green flash, which you can see only with wide open spaces like this, and that's why I didn't see the antelope running by, but rather heard it first. It saw me at the last second and veered away, but it didn't seem very afraid of me, running on by, more intent on making an escape. But an escape from what?

I thought about it for a minute, then didn't think about it at all, which I should have. I should've been aware that an antelope doesn't run like its life depends on it unless its life actually does. Unlike humans, antelope aren't recreational runners, as far as I know.

And if I'd thought about it, I might've moved camp, because only a predator would make an antelope run like that.

I did wonder if someone might be hunting, but there were no roads in the direction it had come from, just empty open desert, and I knew the deep water of the Green River was over the hill beyond where the antelope had come from, blocking anyone from coming in that way.

I made a PBJ sandwich and sat in my chair watching the sunset, which blazed across the far horizon, creating patches of red and gold where the clouds hung low. I then had a nice hot cup of tea, even though the temperature was probably in the 90s.

It was a habit I'd got from my dad, who had always drank hot tea when it was hot, claiming it helped cool him down. My mom was skeptical, until one day my dad showed her an article stating the same thing. After years of her chiding him about it, he was vindicated.

Apparently, your mouth and upper digestive tract have nerves (TRPV1 receptors) that respond to heat, telling your brain to produce more sweat, which then cools you down. The same works for drinking cold drinks on a cold day—though this results in warming you up from making your blood vessels tighten.

Anyway, not to get into a biology lesson here, but drinking the hot tea also always helped me relax. I knew I would sleep well that night, especially after the previous night. I decided to pull out my acoustic guitar, which had been in its case for the entire trip until now.

I'm not the world's greatest guitarist—I just like to strum a bit. It helps me relax and gives me something to do with my hands, the same as fly-fishing. These two things are probably what keep me from being a smoker.

Some Bigfooters hope to draw Bigfoot in by whooping and tree-knocking, but I'd decided to bring my guitar, hoping it might help pique their curiosity. Sure, it's not loud, but I think Bigfoot have very sensitive hearing and know quite well what's going on in their territory. Their survival depends on it.

I'd brought my guitar along, but I'd been too scared to want to encourage any visits. This was the first time I'd played it, and I think the main reason I was playing it now was because I was sure I wasn't even close to Bigfoot territory. There was nothing for them to eat in this barren desert—well, except maybe an antelope or two, but that thought hadn't even crossed my mind. As I mentioned earlier, I was feeling safe and thereby oblivious.

So, I sat there and drank tea and played guitar and watched this most incredible desert sunset and had completely forgotten about the antelope. I was tired, and as the stars came out, I slipped into my tent and lay on top of my bag, as it was too warm to want to sleep inside it.

My tent has a mesh top, the kind you can star gaze through, unless you've covered it up with the rain fly. And that's exactly what I did—lie there and watch the stars unfold in the darkness. I had no fears at all and had soon drifted off to sleep.

But sometime in the middle of the night, I woke up. Something was not right. It was deja vu—I was having a repeat of the night before, up in the meadow where the Howler had maybe wakened me.

I leaned up onto my elbows and listened. What the heck? There was a strange sound right above my tent—it sounded like wings flapping. I lay back down, looking straight up, and I could barely make out a small black object hovering directly above me. It had to be some kind of small bird, but most birds that are nocturnal are owls and such, not small birds like what I was looking at, and few birds are able to hover like that.

It was too large to be a hummingbird. I'd seen hawks hover by flying into the wind and letting it hold them in place, a technique called wind hovering, but there was no wind, and this was no hawk.

I later did some research on hovering birds, and the white-tailed kite is one that can hover like that, but it's territory doesn't include the part of Utah I was in, and they're much larger birds than what I saw. Plus, they're not nocturnal.

After a few minutes, the bird veered off and disappeared, leaving me mystified. Had it maybe been a large bat? I didn't think that bats could hover like that, though later I found out they can.

OK, that in itself was strange, but I was pretty sure it had to have an explanation, though I had no idea at the time what it could be. But in retrospect, the bat idea works, and I really think it was exactly that.

I'd been camped in the desert before and had strange and almost inexplicable things happen. For example, one night I was awakened by a coughing sound coming not too far from where I was sleeping. It sounded just like a person standing nearby, coughing, and it really freaked me out.

After awhile, I managed to get out my headlamp and shine it over to where the sound was coming from, only to see an antelope standing there! It turned and disappeared into the darkness, seeming unafraid.

I've also had antelope come right up to my pickup in broad daylight to see what was going on. Since few people hunt in the desert, I think antelope out there aren't afraid of people and follow their curiosity.

So, this thing had hovered over my tent, and it was probably a bat. But what happened next was no bat.

As I lay there, I could now hear a soft padding sound come up to my tent. It paused, then slowly began walking around my tent, stopping every so often, as if contemplating how to get inside.

At first I thought it must be a coyote, and I was tempted to yell at it and hopefully run it off. Most coyotes are intimidated by humans. But as it continued to pad around my tent, it began to dawn on me that it was way too heavy to be a coyote. There was just something about the way it walked, the soft padding sound, that told me it just couldn't be a coyote.

I was now getting really nervous. It had to be a mountain lion. Had the bat-bird or whatever it was led it to me? Unlikely, and probably just a coincidence. And what was a lion doing out in the desert? There was no prey here, and it was too darn hot. Mountain lions are montane predators. They like cliffs and trees and places they can hide, and they also like deer.

All of a sudden, the running antelope made sense—and the river wasn't very far away, so this mountain lion was probably spending its days by the river hiding from the heat in the big cottonwoods, then hunting by night. Odd as it seemed, it made sense.

All that separated me from a major predator that could easily kill me was a thin wall of nylon, nothing else. But as I lay there, I knew there actually *was* something else—the mountain lion's natural wariness of humans.

Mountain lions are rarely seen, even in areas where the urban interface has pushed into their territory. All the years I'd spent hiking, camping, and fishing in prime lion territory, and I'd never seen one.

The irony of being stalked by a lion in the desert, and even more, while in a tent, hit me. I suspected it had no idea what was in the tent, unless it was used to human smells, so I decided to let it in on the secret, hoping it would leave. I began talking in a low voice.

"Hey, buddy, human in here. Pretty scary stuff."

Silence, then more padding. It was still there. My blood ran a bit cold. Maybe it was a rogue, not afraid of people. Yikes. What to do?

My guitar lay at the foot of my bag, where I had left it. Maybe I could use it to conk the lion over the head if it tried to rip into my tent, which it could easily do. I knew it would be hopeless, but I slowly leaned over and picked up the guitar.

Well, I thought to myself, I'd been wondering what it felt like to live in the time of the sabertooth tiger, and now I was beginning to get a feel for it.

The padding continued, round and round the tent, though slowly.

A thought occurred to me. Had the sabertooth—um, lion—ever heard a guitar? I doubted it. My fingers involuntarily strummed across the strings.

Working up my courage, I began playing an old tune, one of the first I'd ever learned on the guitar. (I'd refused to learn "Stairway to Heaven" like everyone else, as I was my own man.)

I began softly singing, "God gave rock and roll to you, gave rock and roll to you, put it in the soul of everyone..."

I paused. The padding had stopped. For some reason, I felt like the lion had to be standing next to me, mere inches away, just on the other side of the nylon tent wall, listening. I continued singing, my head kind of ducked down just in case.

"Do you know what you want? You don't know for sure. You don't feel right. You can't find a cure..."

I was working up my courage, and I suddenly started screaming the song out, just like Kiss.

"God gave rock and roll to you, gave rock and roll to you, put it in the soul of everyone...yeah yeah yeah!"

I stopped, and it seemed like the words echoed back to me, over and over, but I knew it was my heightened senses. Had playing Kiss been a bit much? Would my screaming make the lion think I wanted to fight? Should I have tried some Bob Marley instead?

I sang, "One love, one love, let's get together and feel all right..."

I stopped, and I heard nothing, no more padding.

I continued sitting there, guitar in hand, listening, until after awhile, I could barely make out a change in the night sky through the thin tent walls. Dawn was just around the corner.

I sat for the longest time, holding my guitar by the neck, ready to whack anything that came ripping into my tent, but the silence was almost overbearing. I knew the lion was gone.

Finally, I unzipped the tent zipper and carefully stuck my head out the door. The sky had lightened enough that I could make out the amorphous shape of my pickup, and I made a run for it, jumping inside and locking the door.

Deja vu all over again, just like the previous night. Here I sat in my truck yet again, scared to death. I felt doomed to never get a good night's sleep. There was no sign of a lion.

When the sun came over the horizon, I got back out and walked to my tent, examining the soft sand around it. There were lion tracks everywhere, and they were huge.

I took several photos with my phone camera and later decided they must've been a good five inches long and five-inches across, based on a quarter I put next to them.

Since the average lion track is about three inches long by three or four inches wide, I knew the creature had been large. And there was no way it was a coyote, as the claws were retracted, which coyotes can't do.

I made coffee, sat in a daze while drinking it, then packed up and headed out.

I stopped at the town park in Green River and took a nap in my truck under the big cottonwoods, then when it started getting too hot, I got onto the freeway and continued my journey.

It had been a long and fearful night, but in thinking about it, the fear had been much different than what I'd felt when I thought I was dealing with Bigfoot.

A mountain lion was actually just as dangerous as any Bigfoot in the sense that it could kill you just as dead. So why the different kind of fear? Bigfoot felt spookier, more terrifying, though I had no idea why. Was it because Bigfoot was more humanlike?

A thought occurred to me—was there maybe something supernatural about Bigfoot? I couldn't answer that question, but somehow I hoped I would find out sooner or later.

5. Sidetracked

· ·

As I drove along the freeway, which was almost free of traffic, I thought once again about what had become almost an obsession—Bigfoot. I wondered if these great creatures were aware of the terror they inspired in me, especially when I was alone in their territory—or, in my case lately, when I was alone about anywhere, whether in Bigfoot country or not.

I was so tired and distracted that I just automatically took the freeway exit a few miles west of the town of Green River, Utah. Before I knew it, I was headed north on a two-lane highway to the small town of Price. I had intended to go straight west and explore some Bigfoot hotspots over on the Wasatch Plateau, a wild area west of Green River.

Once I realized what I'd done, I could've easily turned around, but I decided that I really did want to go north after all. For some reason, I felt a sense of dread at going into that remote stretch of Utah—the Wasatch Plateau has been the location of some of the hairier stories I'd heard.

For example, one was the story of a couple of guys who had gone Bigfooting, only to have one try to tear their camper off their pickup, nearly accomplishing that feat. It was a terrifying tale, and I decided that if I would prefer to have an encounter with a friendly Bigfoot, I might be wise to stay away from that area.

I felt a sense of comfort at now going north, and I realized it was because I wanted to go to Montana, a state I was pretty familiar with, having guided a good many fly-fishing trips there. I love Montana, and I was tired, so it was natural to gravitate towards a place that felt familiar. Plus, like the famous trapper Jim Bridger and all the other mountain men who left their names all over Montana and Wyoming, I was going to have a rendezvous, deep in the Bridger Mountains.

I stopped in Price for gas and coffee, then headed on over the small pass of Soldier Summit, and an hour later dropped down into Spanish Fork, a southern suburb of Salt Lake City. It felt comforting to be in a city, which was an odd feeling for me, as I'm normally allergic to large quantities of people and noise.

As I navigated the rush-hour traffic, my phone rang. It was Sarah. She wanted to know how things were going and was surprised to hear I was in the Salt Lake area. It was good to hear her voice, and I updated her on everything I'd been doing, intentionally neglecting to mention the mountain lion.

I laughed to myself at the irony—hearing about the lion would worry her, whereas hearing about possible Bigfoot vocalizations and other shenanigans didn't seem to bother her a bit.

We'd discussed it many times, and Sarah was of the opinion that Bigfoot didn't exist, but if it did, it was basically harmless. I believed it existed, and I generally held the same opinion about it being harmless—though when I was out alone in the dark woods, I wasn't so sure.

I wanted to talk, but was worried about the heavy traffic, so we cut it short. I would call her later that evening and let her know where my new plans were leading me. I hoped that by then I would have formulated something, but all I knew at that moment was that I was heading to Montana.

It can easily take two long hours to negotiate the freeway from Spanish Fork up to Brigham City, which pretty much covers most of the metropolitan area of Salt Lake City, and that's going a good solid 70 or 80 m.p.h. It's a long stretch of urbanity, and the traffic is often pretty bad.

Not being used to such, I always try to avoid that stretch and Salt Lake City in general, but there I was, white-knuckled and sleep deprived, bumper to bumper with a gazillion drivers madly wanting only to get somewhere else, just like me.

When I got to Brigham City, I was exhausted. I needed a break, but the landscape was pretty barren of camping spots for another hour or two until I got into southern Idaho, and it would soon be dark.

So, on a whim, I took the first exit into Brigham and headed east. I would go visit my old friend Zoey in Logan. There were a few Bigfoot hotspots near there, one being in Logan Canyon at a state park where some kids had spotted one.

Zoey and I go way back, all the way back to Kindergarten, to be exact. We've been friends forever, and when I need a shoulder to cry on or a word of encouragement, if Sarah's not available, Zoey's my next choice.

Zoey works in administration at Utah State University, and she credits me with her finding her true love, Tom, who is now her husband.

Here's the story.

Not long after Sarah and I had been married, we decided we'd like to go cross-country skiing someplace new, having skied what felt like most of Colorado, so we asked Zoey to reserve a weekend for us at the Blind Hollow Yurt up Logan Canyon. The yurt is owned by the university and open only to students and employees.

Well, in order for us to use it, university regulations stated someone affiliated with Utah State University had to be there, so Zoey had to come along, which was fine with us. She reserved it for four, thinking her current boyfriend would want to join us.

Come to find out, he didn't, and to make a long story short, he should have, because our first night there, after skiing in for four miles, we found the yurt already crashed by a lone skier who had gotten himself somewhat lost.

Of course, we let him stay, and he and Zoey hit it off. This was her future husband, Tom, and Zoey says that if we hadn't decided to go on that little weekend getaway, the pair would never have met.

I always get a warm tingle over this story until I wonder what she'll say if they ever get divorced, then I cringe a little.

Anyway, I headed up over Sardine Summit, a small pass over the Wellsville Mountains (and also the site of a few

Bigfoot encounters), and was soon coming down the other side to the twinkling lights of Logan. I'd tried to call Zoey and nobody was home, but I knew I'd be welcome. Zoey was like the sister I never had.

I pulled into the drive of Zoey and Tom's little bungalow, but it looked pretty forlorn there in the dark with no lights on. Now, I was worried. They appeared to be out of town.

Chalk another one up for what I call serendipity but what should instead maybe be called stupidity—I then realized I should have called a few days ahead. But how can you call ahead when you don't know where you're going or when you'll be there?

Just then, their neighbor, Mia, drove up. I walked over to talk to her. I knew Mia and her husband from previous visits, and we'd even had dinner together several times at Zoey's, so I was no stranger.

Mia informed me that Zoey and Tom had gone off to Jamaica for a two-week vacation, but were scheduled to return day after tomorrow. Mia seemed to sense that I was lost and said I could stay at her house until then if I wanted.

I was crestfallen. I didn't want to stay with Mia's family and impose, but I didn't want to camp, either. I'd have to drive up Logan Canyon, and it was too late to find a spot in what I knew were busy campgrounds.

I asked Mia if she would mind having me camped next door in Zoey's back yard, as I knew Zoey wouldn't care. Mia said that was fine by her, so I opened the back gate and set up my camp chair and sleeping gear. I wouldn't need a tent, as the yard was very private, surrounded by trees and a privacy fence, and I could sleep on their back deck.

It was kind of weird being there, camped behind a house, yet it felt safe and secure—no Bigfoot or mountain lions. And even though I was tired, the night was young, so I drove a few blocks over to a restaurant and had a few beers along with an oven-fired pizza.

It was all good, and after calling Sarah, I slept like a baby that night, awakening the next morning on the shaded deck to the peaceful cooing sound of mourning doves, with Bigfoot the last thing on my mind.

6. Bigfoot Folklore

· ·

The next day, as I sat on Zoey and Tom's back deck, drinking an espresso I'd gotten on nearby Main Street at a place called Jitters, I again examined my journey, or what there was of it so far, anyway.

I'd been out well over a week, and I'd had some odd things happen, but nothing definitively Bigfoot. Were my fears of Bigfoot becoming a self-fulfilling prophecy? Was I somehow jinxing my own expedition somehow? Would I end up not having an encounter, or would I meet the most fearsome Bigfoot ever, just because I was half-expecting it?

I didn't think so. In fact, I really didn't believe I had any control at all over such things. The only thing I had control over were my own actions, and believing something existed didn't make it so. To think something was real based on shadows and feelings was just too spurious, an idea based on faulty reasoning.

But what about the idea that Bigfoot might be supernatural? I'd read plenty of Bigfoot accounts that had supernatural elements, like weird blue lights, cars not starting, tracks stopping in mid-stride, people hearing Bigfoot voices in their heads, and strange UFO-like sightings, just to name a few.

But if Bigfoot had supernatural powers (and remember, supernatural simply means something beyond scientific understanding or the laws of nature), couldn't it somehow sense what I was feeling and act accordingly? Could it sense my obsession with it—and would I thereby somehow attract it to me? Or maybe the opposite, make it avoid me?

Once again, I didn't think so. I'd never felt Bigfoot was anything beyond a very elusive primate, one so smart it had managed to elude human capture—a very clever creature, but a very real one held to the same physical laws I was. I didn't think Bigfoot could read minds, and I didn't think there was anything paranormal about the creature at all.

Mia had said Zoey and Tom would be back soon, and I really wanted to see them, since I was there already. I decided to stay a few days and see what I could come up with. I would spend the day in Logan, then maybe go up the canyon and camp for a night, coming back and meeting up with Zoey and Tom the next day.

I then recalled a fishing client a few years back who was enthralled with Bigfoot, and I wonder in retrospect if my Bigfoot books weren't what actually made her sign up for a fly-fishing trip. She seemed more interested in talking about Bigfoot than learning how to fish.

Her name was Diana and she was studying folklore at Utah State University in Logan, though I suspected she had graduated since then. We'd spent some time talking about Bigfoot as folklore, and she told me about the Fife Folklore Archives at the university, one of the country's largest repositories.

I decided to see what I could find there about Bigfoot. I knew that anyone could access the information at the university library, and it sounded like a great way to spend a few hours. So, I got into my truck and headed up the hill to the campus, which was easy to find—just look for the Old Main spire with the big A for Aggies.

I was soon ensconced in the library, which was a unique feeling for me, as I hadn't been in one since I was in college a number of years back. I started looking through the folklore collections, finally selecting the one titled "Supernatural Folklore."

The human mind is pretty creative, and I was amazed at the number and variety of things people had come up with. It was a pretty fascinating bunch of stories. I had to look up the definition of folklore, and it's basically the traditional beliefs, legends, and customs of a group that are passed down by word of mouth.

Here are a few examples of what I found—though not Bigfoot related—titles of folklore tales:

House never finished being built is now "building itself."

Two boys have no recollection of switching sides in bed during the night.

Lady in white appears in Logan Canyon.

Man taking shelter in cave finds large city inside, but can't find the cave again later.

Devil rock shakes when youth tries to climb it against warnings not to.

Men sleep in car along roadside and wake up in a different country.

Airplane touches down and chases car along road.

Train's engine number changes as family drives past it.

Mysterious footprints in snow allow a young girl to avoid ruining her only pair of shoes.

Old ghost people seen peeing.

Death in family happens every time a chicken shows up.

And on and on. It was pretty entertaining, to say the least. But I then came to these:

Hairy 12-foot Wasatch Monster thought to live in North Canyon, Utah.

An unknown white and massive creature attacks men while camping in Idaho.

Red-eyed, hairy monster appears at campsite in Providence Canyon, Utah.

Foul-smelling monster enters home and chases family member who is alone in house.

Bigfoot shows himself to those individuals who he feels are ready to see him.

Creature thought to exist in Dry Canyon near Logan, Utah.

That last one really caught my eye. I was unable to read any of the actual accounts, however, as the person who was in charge of the special collections was gone, and all I could access was the index, leaving me disappointed, though thoroughly entertained.

After spending a couple of hours in the library, I was ready to get back out into the fresh air and sunlight. But first, I had something I needed to check out—where was Dry Canyon? It was supposedly somewhere near Logan.

I sat down at a computer carousel and did a search. Sure enough, there was a Dry Canyon nearby, just across town. It looked pretty easy to find—right at the end of Center Street.

I went outside. Since the campus was on a hill, I could stand and actually make out the canyon's entrance. It was less than a mile away. I now knew what I would be doing for the rest of the day.

7. Dry Canyon

I went back to Zoey's and gathered a few things in my day-pack—water, snacks, my camera, a jacket, and a flashlight. Dry Canyon was my destination, but the day was getting on and I didn't have a lot of time before dark. I'm guessing it was about two in the afternoon, and even though the summer days were long, I wanted to be back out well before sunset.

In retrospect, my major error was not finding a map to study, which I always do before going into the backcountry. That way, I get a visual image of the lay of the land and where trails run, as well as major drainages. I guess I figured since the trailhead was basically in a residential neighborhood (called River Heights) that any trail would be well-trodden and easy to follow.

This did prove to be the case, and I would've been fine if I'd taken the same route out that I took in. My grandpa used to say that you're never lost, you're just breaking new trails, so maybe I could say that in this case. I was on a trail the entire time coming back—it just wasn't the trail I wanted to be on.

Since all the drainages pour into the Cache Valley, where Logan lies, I knew all I would have to do is go downhill if I needed out. But I was backcountry savvy enough to know that some drainages are easier to follow than others—and some have rivers one has to cross, as well as impenetrable thickets of willows and underbrush. I could tell even from a distance that the Bear River Mountains had some pretty thick underbrush, and I knew Cache Valley was a pretty big place.

I guess you now know where this story is heading. I did get lost later, in a sense, but I never once left the trail, even though it turned into a road. I was heading downhill and I knew I would eventually come out into the Cache Valley, but I had no idea when or how. This wasn't my first trek into the Bear River Mountains, but it would be my first at night, and I hope it was the last night hike I take anywhere.

Since I hadn't been able to access the Bigfoot story while in the library, all I knew was that someone had claimed to have had a Bigfoot encounter somewhere in Dry Canyon near Logan. What the nature of that encounter was, I had no idea. It could've been anything from hearing a questionable sound to a full-on run-in.

My plan to stick to what I knew were Bigfoot hotspots was now totally sidetracked. But what was new? Nothing else was going as planned. I hadn't even planned on being in Logan.

My plans had shifted in a big way. I had planned to visit some of the more recognized Bigfoot lairs and work my way from iconic spot to spot, much like a photographer who travels from national park to national park would do, except I would hopefully be documenting Bigfoot instead of famous landmarks. My list included places where Bigfoot had been seen or heard several times, but that plan was now history.

I slowly negotiated the traffic on Main Street in Logan (some of the worst I'd ever seen) and on up into the subdivision where the Dry Canyon Trail started on the upper bench of what was once the shoreline of ancient Lake Bonneville. From there, the trail would climb 4,000 feet in four miles to the summit of Logan Peak at 9711 feet, skirting along a ridge called the Syncline Bench for a ways.

I did know that the trail split at one point and the other branch dropped down into Logan Canyon, the next major drainage to the north. No way did I want to end up there, as I knew how steep the canyon walls were. I simply wanted to hike the trail as long as I felt comfortable doing so, then hightail it back to my truck before dark. I figured I'd go a couple of miles and then turn around.

I parked my pickup at the trailhead, then began a leisurely walk. Jagged gray pinnacles and spires guarded the canyon entrance, giving the place a kind of ominous feeling. It wasn't long before I'd covered a couple of miles, as the trail was fairly easy. I hadn't met anyone coming down, but that didn't surprise me, since it was a week day and most folks were probably working.

Now, in what I estimated to be the third mile, the trail suddenly began switchbacking up a steep hill, back and forth. It had gone from a low moderate to fairly strenuous hike in a very short distance. Whereas I'd been hiking through bigtooth maples, it was now becoming aspen, and I could see that it turned into fir and pine higher up.

··· 5 7 ···

As I topped a ridge, I could see the trail veering off towards Logan Canyon. The internet site I'd read said there was a spring along the trail, so I kept going along, even though I knew I'd have to backtrack.

Sure enough, I soon came upon a spring with a pipe sticking out. The water was cool and clear, and since my water bottle was almost empty, I filled it, drank a bunch, then filled it again. I leaned against a tree and tried to catch my breath, listening. If there were Bigfoot around, they probably used this very same spring.

I looked around for tracks, but found nothing, so I turned and started backtracking up the trail. I could see what looked like the top of Logan Peak, but I could also see that the sun was beginning to look pretty low in the sky. My cellphone said it was six p.m., so I figured I had only a couple of hours of daylight left.

I don't know what I was thinking, or, to be honest, I don't think I was thinking, but I decided I wanted to get to that summit. It was kind of a compulsion, a feeling that since I'd made it that far, it would be a shame not to get to the top and take in the view. It was that same kind of compulsion that has left a good many climbers injured or worse.

I knew I'd basically have to run back if I carried out my plan, but going downhill wasn't too bad, and I did have a flashlight, and so far, it had been a pretty good trail, one that wouldn't be too hard to negotiate at dusk. I figured I could make the summit in less than an hour.

So, since the internet hiking guide had said there was no real trail up to the summit, I left the known trail and started bushwhacking through the trees. I soon veered as far out of them as I could because of all the deadfall, which made the going hard. I kind of cut across the head of the canyon, then worked my way around, and I can say it was much steeper than it had looked. Something kept telling me to turn around, but I stupidly ignored it.

I was soon on top, panting and sweating. I drank half of my water and ate a granola bar while taking in the majestic views from near several big communication towers and a microwave building with a sign that read, "This site under video surveillance."

I could see most of Cache Valley and across to the beautiful rugged Wellsville Mountains, as well as many of the small towns surrounding Logan. Behind me, I could see the vast slopes of the Naomi Wilderness.

And I will tell you this, it was worth the climb, just as I knew it would be. It was a stunning view, and one I'll never forget. And I'll also never forget seeing a few big snow-fields and suddenly realizing that it would be cold up there at night—and it was almost night.

And I'll also never forget the feeling I had knowing I could never find my way back down that lush canyon in the dark, even with a flashlight, for I had no idea where the trail was that I'd left behind when I'd left it to bushwhack up the slope.

As the sun began to set, what had been a light breeze quickly turned into a stiff wind. I put on my jacket and immediately knew I was unprepared to spend the night up there.

I pulled my jacket close around me and shivered, wondering what I should do next.

8. Logan Peak

As the sun quickly dropped over the far ridges of the rugged Wellsville Mountains, I knew I had to act quickly. Even in the summer, mountain temperatures can get cold enough to give you hypothermia, and Logan Peak was only a few hundred feet shy of 10,000 feet.

Could I find enough wood to build a fire that would last all night? There were plenty of trees around, but I quickly realized there was no way I could gather enough wood for the night, especially since most of it would need splitting.

The top of the peak was accessed by a road for the communications towers, and I stood there, wondering how long it would take to traverse back down. I knew it would have to zigzag a lot to climb the steep mountain, but did it then follow some canyon for miles and miles once it was down off the mountain slopes?

That was when I realized in full my folly at not studying a map. If I had, I would've noted any such routes just in case I needed to take them. But I hadn't. Now the temperatures were quickly dropping with a colder wind chill setting in.

I had to make a quick decision. I knew the rough road would eventually get me back to civilization, even if I had to walk all night, and I also knew I had no choice but to get down off the top of the peak. Once I got lower, I knew the winds would be tempered, if not stop entirely, and I also knew that walking would keep me warm. I really didn't have much of a choice—walk down this side on a road or bushwhack back down the side I'd come up and promptly get lost.

I drank the rest of my water under the theory that it's better *in* you than *on* you, buttoned up my jacket, got out my flashlight, and started off down the road at a fast jog. I needed to make good time while I could still see.

Once it was dark, I could use my flashlight, but only in moderation, for the batteries would only last a few hours. I tried not to feel too desolate, but I knew it would be a long night, and I was already tired.

I was quickly off the top, but soon had to slow down, as I was getting winded. The long hike up had taken its toll. The jog turned into a fast power walk, and I estimated I was a good mile from the top when I passed a small lake. I thought about filling my water bottle, but the thought of giardia stopped me. Soon, it was dark enough that I had to use my flashlight.

I was glad I'd gotten as far as I had, as there were several side roads that would've been totally confusing in the dark. As it was, I managed to stay on the main road, which seemed to be going pretty much south at this point.

I found out later that the road was called Canyon Road and went down what's called Millville Canyon, skirting the towering Millville Peak. It came out in the little town of Millville, near Logan, but it was a long ways.

There's nothing quite like hiking in the dark along a road you've never been on in country you know nothing about. It's kind of a helpless feeling, and all you can do is keep moving forward.

I would turn on my light just long enough to assess the road for a hundred feet or so, hike in the dark, then turn the light back on for a moment for the next stretch. And all the while, I was trying to make good time, but getting more and more fatigued. At least I was now down out of the wind, and the road seemed to level out some, even though I was still obviously going downhill. I seemed to be following a drainage.

I had walked what I guessed to be several miles when the road began zigzagging again, and I could tell I was dropping down off the side of the mountain into yet another drainage. I was now exhausted and sat down on a rock to rest.

As I set there in the dark, I thought I could hear something coming up the road behind me, as if following me, unaware that I had stopped. I immediately thought of the mountain lion I'd heard in my camp back in the desert, but I knew a lion was a stalker and I would be totally unaware of its presence. This had to be something else.

I slipped down a bit behind the rock, on alert and scared. Of course, Bigfoot was the next thing that crossed my mind, and I wasn't so sure this was the time and place I wanted to meet one, the purpose of my expedition notwithstanding. I was exhausted and cold and felt very vulnerable alone there on the massive flanks of the Bear River Mountains.

It came closer, seemingly not too worried about making noise, as I could hear it stepping on twigs and dry grasses. I tried to make myself smaller down behind that rock, but I knew I was prime game for any predator. I didn't even have my trusty pocket knife along, as I'd left it in my pickup. I held my breath.

Now it seemed to stop only a dozen feet away. I sat there, all hunched down, and whatever it was, it stood there, unafraid.

After a few minutes of this, I began to feel desperate. I was so tired, so lost, so hungry—and the last thing I needed was to be so scared. I decided I would go down fighting. I stood up, shining my flashlight directly at whatever it was and yelled at the top of my lungs, "Go away, you stupid SOB!"

A young buck stood about 20 feet away. Its eyes were big and it looked stunned, just as scared as I'd been, now that it could see what its curiosity had gotten it into. It quickly turned and bolted into the darkness.

I began laughing, which soon turned into a sobbing. I couldn't help myself—it was a form of release. I had so much pent-up tension. I was exhausted, and I really wasn't sure if I would get out of this one alive.

After a few moments, I sat back down on the rock. I felt better, letting off all that steam or whatever you would call it. I leaned back and tried to get a grip on myself, to critically assess the situation again.

I was now low enough in altitude that the night was just chilly, not really all that cold, so I knew I probably wouldn't die of hypothermia. My flashlight seemed to be holding up well, so I could keep going if I wanted, but maybe it would be better to just stay where I was and get some rest.

I could tell from the position of the Big Dipper that it was near 2 a.m. I pulled my jacket around me—if I could get some rest, I could continue my hike out in the daylight.

I then realized how thirsty I was, not to mention hungry. I'd been hungry before and would survive that one, but being thirsty was bad. I wished then I'd filled my water bottle up at the little lake. Better to get giardia than to die of dehydration.

I sat there, leaning against that rock, for what seemed like forever, unable to sleep, as my legs started to cramp up. Too much walking. I was in pretty good shape, but I figured I'd hiked for at least a good 12 hours at that point, some of it bushwhacking, gaining 4,000 feet in elevation and dropping at least half that, if not more.

I had managed to drift off when I woke with a start. I thought I could hear an engine in the distance. I listened again carefully. Yes, it was definitely an engine, and it was getting closer. It sounded like an ATV, and now I could see its lights, but it wasn't on the road I was on and seemed to be a bit farther south.

I quickly realized that there must be another road that met this one, but ahead of where I was. The ATV was going to miss me. I got up, turned on my light, and started running down the road, trying to get to where the two roads must merge.

I was too late. It hadn't seen me and had indeed merged onto my road, but about a hundred feet ahead of me. I could hear the sound fading into the distance, the ATV's tail lights seemingly taunting me.

What was someone on an ATV doing out this time of night? Poaching deer? If so, I was probably better off not getting a ride.

I stood by the road, my legs cramping even more. But now I could hear the ATV again—it was coming back! I flashed my light, and soon it pulled up next to me, a four-seater with two men in the front. They had seen my light and decided to turn around and see what was going on, even though it had spooked them. I could understand this in light of what they later told me.

I was soon on my way down the road, and I can't recall ever being so happy to get a ride. They filled my water bottle several times before I stopped feeling so thirsty. We wound down that rough dirt road quite a ways before emerging from the canyon into the tiny town of Millville. I would've had quite a walk out the next day if they hadn't seen me. With no water, it would've been a tough go.

I helped them load their ATV in the dark, and since they were from Smithfield, just north of Logan, they gave me a ride all the way home. I would go get my pickup later.

They were local bowhunters who'd been scouting out the country for deer season, even though it was a month or more away. They'd decided to scout out a rough drainage on foot, and like me, had managed to get themselves a bit lost.

They'd finally reconnected with their ATV and headed home on a side road that connected to the road I'd been on.

They tried to explain it all, saying they'd been up the Left Fork of Blacksmith Canyon, but I was kind of lost without a frame of reference.

Later, I would check it out on a map and see that they'd been close to the Hardware Ranch, an elk refuge and also the site of several Bigfoot sightings, including tracks with a huge stride of over 11 feet.

It was 5 a.m. when they let me off at Zoey's, and I stumbled into the back yard and crawled into my sleeping bag, clothes and all, where I immediately fell into a deep sleep, dreaming of the huge dark figure they said had followed them the whole time they'd been lost.

It could have been Bigfoot or about anything, including an elk or moose. But in spite of my quest for Bigfoot, whatever it was, I was glad it had followed them, not me.

9. Logan Canyon

. . . .

I knew when I woke it was late. Sunlight was filtering through the leaves of the big elm in Zoey's back yard, and I'd been dreaming I was drinking a coconut spritzer while sitting on a white-sands tropical beach. It was one of the nicer dreams I'd ever had, leaving me with a peaceful feeling.

As I woke, I realized I was very thirsty, so I got up and turned on the garden hose, drinking from it and then splashing my face with water. I was still dehydrated from yesterday, and I realized I was also famished. All I'd eaten since starting my hike yesterday was a granola bar.

My legs were stiff and sore, but I knew the best way to loosen them up was to go for a walk—the hair of the dog cure, so they say. I needed to get my pickup, which was at least a mile away. Mia had gone to work much earlier, so no free ride there.

I put on some clean clothes, grabbed my keys, and started walking, stopping at a little nearby espresso cafe called Cafe Ibis, where I got a triple shot espresso and a sandwich. I then walked to Center Street and headed towards the mountains. The flanks of Logan Peak stood high above, and it was hard to believe I'd been way up there just yesterday.

As I trudged up the steep hill through River Heights, I marveled at how close the town sat to wilderness. Just literally right across the street from the houses were thick stands of box elder, maple, and scrub oak. I wondered if Bigfoot ever sat up there watching the town, wondering what the human species was up to next, shaking his or her head in wonder.

My pickup was just as I'd left it, and I was soon back at Zoey's, having stopped at the grocery store on the way back, picking up a six-pack of beer and some stuff for a barbecue.

Mia had said Zoey and Tom would return that day, and I figured I'd wrestle up a nice dinner for them. It was now mid-afternoon, so I expected them any time.

Sure enough, it wasn't long before their little Honda pulled into the drive and they spilled out, accompanied by a dog that looked to be a young black lab.

They seemed really surprised to see me, though Zoey told me nothing I did ever surprised her, whatever that meant—but she was smiling, at least. She also commented on how I looked like I'd been run over by a truck, but other than that, they seemed happy to see me, and more than happy to have a nice dinner waiting.

The new dog was named Zadie, and they'd rescued her just a few months ago from the local shelter. She'd been in a doggie daycare while they were on vacation. Zadie and I were soon best friends, especially since she smelled the ribs I was barbecuing on the grill. I managed to slip her a few bites, which made her like me even more.

I won't bore you with the story of my next two days of domesticity, especially since there isn't a story. All I did was sleep and drink and eat and hang out with Zoey and Tom and Zadie. And I had plenty of the Blue Mountain coffee they'd brought back from their Jamaican trip.

It was nice, but I eventually realized I needed to get back on the Bigfoot trail. Zoey thought it was kind of funny that I'd taken this expedition upon myself (she didn't believe in Bigfoot for one minute), and Tom seemed a bit worried about me (I think he was more of a believer but wouldn't admit it).

Finally, after recovering from my trek and feeling like I was wearing out my welcome, I said my goodbye and was on my way, though I was once again unsure of where I was going.

I knew I was eventually going to Montana, but should I first spend some time in Wyoming? I was less than 200 miles from Jackson Hole and the Grand Tetons, which was some pretty wild country. If I went there, I would be very close to Yellowstone and the region where the legendary Yellowstone ranger, Action Jackson, had seen Bigfoot several times.

Jackson had since retired, but I felt he was a very credible person and wouldn't lie about such. Yellowstone would be a great place for Bigfoot—they could soak in the hot springs in the winter and have the place all to themselves—along with a few gazillion buffalo, moose, grizzly bears, and wolves, that is.

I didn't decide where I was going until I got in my truck

and left Zoey's drive. Lo and behold, Main Street wasn't as crazy as usual, and I was able to make a left turn, which determined my course of action for the next part of my trip. I thought this was kind of sad, not being able to even plan which direction I should go, but there you have it.

If traffic had been bad, I would've turned right and headed on back to I-15 and Montana. Instead, it looked like I was headed to Wyoming. Such are the ways of chance and serendipity—and indecision.

I would take the back highway to Jackson Hole, which meant I would go through Logan Canyon on up to Garden City and Bear Lake, then cross over the bottom corner of Idaho. It was a gorgeous drive, much prettier than the drive up I-15, and probably the real reason I turned left instead of right, as opposed to some mysterious subconscious voice saying "Go left, young man."

Besides, by going left, I would go directly by Cafe Ibis again, and I wanted another coffee, which is a force that seems to have driven a good portion of my life, if you were to ask Sarah (though instead of saying *force*, she would say *addiction*).

I was soon climbing the hill by campus, coffee in hand (another triple shot), and I thought about my time sitting there in the library the other day, no idea that I would soon be lost on the top of Logan Peak.

Life was like that, things seemed to happen and then work out, no matter where you went or what you did. You just had to keep it all in perspective. I hadn't accomplished much of anything, but I was still alive, wasn't I? That seemed like enough of an accomplishment, given the circumstances.

Logan Canyon starts immediately past the campus and is bisected by a two-lane highway that's a designated Utah Scenic Byway. The road winds through thick vegetation flanked by huge cliffs of gray dolomite and limestone, with occasional caves and sinks, as well as a number of state campgrounds nestled between the small river and the huge impressive cliffs.

I missed Zadie. I thought again about getting a dog. Maybe when I got back home Sarah and I could discuss it. Or maybe I could just get one, leaving nothing open for discussion, as I knew my wife wouldn't argue if I wanted one.

I just wasn't sure how a dog would fit into our lives and needed to think about it more. But I'd sure had fun playing with that silly black Lab, and I remembered how much I'd enjoyed hanging with Mark's Corgi, Ginger, back forever ago.

The Logan River sparkled in the afternoon sun, and I wanted to stop and fish, but I knew I would soon be totally sidetracked if I did, and besides, I didn't have a Utah license, though that wouldn't stop me later. I half expected to come around a curve in the canyon and see a Bigfoot, it seemed like such good habitat.

After a good 20 miles or so, I started climbing out of the canyon and could see what's called the Sinks to my right, an area where water had eroded the underground limestone, eventually creating caves that collapsed, in turn leaving huge depressions shaped like giant bathtubs, some over a mile long.

It was a popular snowmobile area in winter, and one of the sinks, Peter Sinks, held the Utah record for the coldest temperature in Utah, at -69F. The big bathtubs actually dammed the cold air, and it could be 20 degrees colder at the bottom than at the lip of the tub. Sometimes even just a few steps down from the sink's lip would see temperatures drop 15 degrees.

Anyway, I kept going, topping out at the summit near Tony Grove, a popular camping area. Not far to my left were the slopes of Beaver Mountain, a popular ski area, and I could soon see the beautiful Mediterranean-blue waters of Bear Lake far ahead and below, the color coming from the reflection of the limestone particles suspended in the water, much like the pale-blue colors seen in glacial lakes from suspended glacial till. Bear Lake was called the Mediterranean of the Rockies because of this color.

I would soon be in Garden City, one of Utah's best-kept secrets, sitting along the shores of Bear Lake like a small gem on a crown. I could see across the lake, which was formed by an earthquake and was about 20 miles long and eight wide, and the distant white sands sparkled in the afternoon sun. I wanted to be there, just like that beach in my dream, lounging around and drinking coconut spritzers, if there even were such a thing.

The near shores of the lake were a swampy bird refuge, for the most part, or private land, and far across the lake I could see a few sailboats. My plans were changing by the moment.

I suddenly knew I had to go to the far shores of Bear Lake. I had no idea why, but it was just something that appealed to me, right then and there.

How I would get there, I had no idea.

10. The Bear Lake Monster

· ·

I came down the long grade that led to Garden City (which is actually about as far from being a city as one can get), when I suddenly slammed on my brakes.

There, sitting by a gas station, was exactly what I'd been searching for ever since I got my old Ford pickup several years ago—a topper I could actually afford. The sign said it was $150, and it looked like it might fit.

I went inside, asked about it, and was soon bolting it onto my pickup rails with the help of the gas-station manager. Before long, I was back on the road, my white truck now sporting a kind of beat-up but perfectly functional red fiberglass topper with two opening side windows (that I later found out wouldn't open), a window that opened into the back window of my cab (which did open), and a big pull-up door on the back.

No matter that it bore a sticker that read, "Half Deputy, Half Rock Star," and another that read, "I Shot the Sheriff." I was styling.

I'd wanted a topper for some time, but usually they were out of my price range or didn't fit my truck. Now I could keep my stuff locked up in the back and not worry about it getting stolen or rained on. In fact, I could even sleep back there now, if I wanted, which seemed to go along with my current modus operandi of hiding out from Bigfoot.

I suddenly felt much more secure and decided I would keep my eye out for a cheap mattress to put back there. Might as well be comfortable, as well as warm and dry.

Next, I impetuously pulled over at a little tourist shop that had the word "Fudge" in huge letters, something that I would usually never buy, as I usually answered to my wife and her health-conscious ways.

But what Sarah didn't know wouldn't hurt her, and I figured I'd earned a bit of sugar after my long hike down off Logan Peak. I emerged from the shop with a box of vanilla macadamia-nut fudge, a bag of Bear Lake saltwater taffy (I wasn't sure how that worked, as it was a freshwater lake), and a raspberry shake—enough sugar to put me in the ER, if I ate it all at once, which I was tempted to do.

The gas-station guy had also given me a map, and I now knew how to get to the other side of the lake. I drove by the marina for the Bear Lake State Park and thought about stopping at the beach there until I saw it was a fee area. I wouldn't be able to pay too many fees now that I'd bought the topper. I'd have to be really frugal, and the sugar binge would have to last me for awhile.

Bear Lake was the site of several mountain man gather-ings or rendezvous back in the early days of the 1800s, and, in fact, that's how the Cache Valley got its name—from the trappers caching their furs there. Jim Bridger must've been a big wig at the party, for it seemed that everything around has his name associated with it—I was in Bridgerland.

All along the lake were pretty cottages and camp-grounds, and even though it was a week day, there seemed to be plenty of tourists around. I figured the east shore would be primitive and hard to get to and thereby not see many people. I was planning on camping there for the night.

I really don't know where I got the idea it would be deserted, but I would turn out to be way wrong.

As I drove along the lakeshore, I wondered where the Bear Lake monster was today. I'd been told to watch out for it by the guy at the gas station, and even though he laughed, he acted like he was almost serious. He spent some time telling me about it while we were putting on the topper.

Seems that this thing had been seen by folks for years and was kind of like the Loch Ness monster, except maybe bigger and more aggressive and able to come out of the water for short distances and chase people.

Its early sightings were corroborated by several staunch Mormons with good credentials and who would never lie, according to their followers. In fact, the early settlers said they'd heard of the monster from the earlier Shoshone Indians, so this thing supposedly went way back.

I found out later that the whole thing had been a hoax by one of the Mormon brethren named Joseph C. Rich, possibly as an attempt to bring more business to the area, where he owned a store. The county Bear Lake is in is now named for him, Rich County. He even admitted in print to perpetuating the hoax, but by then, the folklore was deeply entrenched and the Bear Lake communities were running with it, holding monster days and parades and such.

But at the time I was there, I had no idea it was all fabricated, and even though I didn't believe in it, it still left me feeling a bit on edge that night, camped on the beach. But I'm getting ahead of myself here.

I was now following the lake shore back north, having come around the south end. The shoreline was interspersed with vacation houses and fields—at least where there was room for such, as in many places steep hills came right down to the water, barely leaving room for the highway.

I finally came to a park with a boat ramp and stopped. There wasn't much of a beach, so I took a quick break and then continued on. Shortly after that, I came to a bigger beach, so I decided this would be my stop for the night.

The terrain was rocky, and one could tell from the color of the water that the edge quickly dropped off. The gas station guy had told me that the east shore was sometimes used by scuba divers, as it dropped to over 200 feet deep in a very short distance. It was a good place to scuba dive, assuming there were no lake monsters.

I pulled out onto the beach a short distance and got out my camp chair and a can of beer. I was tired, even though I hadn't driven all that far. Bear Lake was only about 60 miles or so from Logan.

As I set there, watching a dramatic red sunset over the Bear River Mountains to the west, I thought more about the folklore articles I'd read at the university library. Folklore was definitely something that came from deep in the human psyche, but why?

Did we puny humans need a way to keep ourselves from getting into more trouble than we already did? Was making up scary and weird stories and then proceeding as if they were real our preferred method for scaring each other away from wild and dark places? Many cultures have tales of bogeymen that are used to keep children from wandering too far. Was Bigfoot such a tale?

The longer I sat there and thought about it, the more my skepticism began to kick in, and I wondered if the literally thousands of reported Bigfoot sightings all over North America were bogus.

Were there really that many people who would hoax and outright lie about Bigfoot? And sure, now that people can read accounts on the internet and easily make their stories sound real by borrowing details from other stories, what about all those accounts before the internet?

These older reports seemed to me to be of a creature that had to exist, otherwise why would someone in California report seeing a creature that looked exactly like one seen in Alberta? There wasn't any way to corroborate accounts back then, so why were all the sightings so similar, regardless of where they took place?

I leaned back and watched the waves pick up a bit from the evening breeze and imagined for a second I could see a big head way out there, something that quickly dipped back into the waters—probably the Bear Lake Monster.

I laughed at myself. It was more likely just a whitecap. We humans are good at making things look like predators.

It's deep in our genetic makeup, and we look for patterns in things to help us to quickly determine if they're dangerous or not. Some of it's also cultural. For example, if you're not a Catholic, you're way less inclined to see a picture of Mother Mary on a piece of toast.

OK, I could understand why I might mistake a wave for a monster's head, and it made sense that many Bigfoot seen in the woods are just leaves or branches or even stumps that look vaguely monster-like.

I recalled one climber somewhere in the Himalayas who actually saw and photographed a Yeti standing waiting for him to come down the trail. He stood there for a long time, and it didn't move, so he finally retreated, spooked.

That photo created a lot of commentary until eventually another hiker retraced his path and discovered it was just a rock outcropping. The first hiker seemed genuine in thinking it was a Yeti and seemed relieved to find it wasn't.

But what about accounts where someone sees a Bigfoot actually running across a field or moving? For example, what about the pilot of a private plane that saw a large hairy creature trudging through deep snow in Utah's High Uintas?

He didn't just see something that could maybe be a Bigfoot, he actually saw a large hairy creature trudging through the deep snow. This happened in 1980, long before the internet existed, and not too far from Bear Lake as the crow flies. Could it have been a bear? Maybe, but most bears are deep in hibernation by the time there's deep snow, and they don't walk on two legs.

Many Bigfoot accounts have a lot of detail and even include a sound component, which goes beyond Bigfoot sightings resulting from the human mind trying to create meaningful patterns. Sure, some people have no compunctions about hoaxing, but I felt that the sheer number of sightings had to increase the possibility that there was a real creature out there somewhere.

All it would take is one real sighting for Bigfoot to be real. I suddenly wanted that sighting to be mine, scary or not.

The sun had now set, and it was soon pitch dark. I pulled out my pad and sleeping bag and placed them on the beach. I hadn't been on a real beach for many years, and the quiet lapping of the waves soon lulled me to sleep.

I awoke sometime in the night to go pee, the beer taking its toll, and as I stood there, looking out at the newly risen half-moon's light glimmering across the lake, I thought I saw something long and sinuous slipping across the waters.

It was probably just a log, I thought, grabbing my bag and crawling into the back of my pickup. I pulled the door of the topper closed and locked it with an almost tangible feeling of security.

11. The High Uintas

I don't know why, but I've always been drawn to wildlands and places where people are few and far between. Maybe it stems from childhood influences and how I was raised, but it's a feeling I've always had.

Anyway, I woke the next morning to a beautiful blue sky, Bear Lake dotted with white sailboats in the distance. It was like something on a postcard, and yet I suddenly wanted to be far away, far from the pretty cottages and tourists and supposed lake monster, though I seriously doubted its existence.

I needed some wide-open spaces, places where one could wander for miles and never see any sign of human activity. And I knew where that place would be—Utah's High Uinta Mountains.

I'd had an interest in the Uintas for many years, but I'd never done much hiking there, in spite of them being almost in my back yard, only a hundred miles more or less from home. I'd spent a lot of time reading Bigfoot sightings there and heard a few stories told around campfires, and

I'd always wanted to go spend time in that beautiful range.

I drove back onto the Eastshore Highway, retracing my route from yesterday, the whole time trying to decide if I really should go to the Uintas or not. I could just as easily head back to Logan, then get onto the freeway and head north.

The Uintas were the number one place for Bigfoot sightings in Utah—definitely a Bigfoot hotspot—but it would mean backtracking a good 150 miles southeast, far off my route up to Montana. But I was in good company, as Bigfoot was never on track—most accounts indicated the creature was usually seen when least expected.

When I reached the end of the lake, I headed south— it looked like I was going to the Uintas—and was soon in Laketown. According to my map, the quickest way was to continue southeast into Wyoming and head on down to Evanston. Once there, I had several options, depending on which part of the Uintas I decided to visit.

The road I was on was more of a backroad than a highway, and I saw very little traffic. As I drove along, I thought about the numerous Bigfoot sightings in the Uintas, including the one mentioned earlier where the pilot saw a black hairy manlike creature in the snow. That was just one of many.

Accounts of Bigfoot in the Uintas go way back, including eighteen-inch footprints found near Hoyt Peak in 1976, and another account from the 1980s where two Utah men tried to imitate a Bigfoot call and were answered by what they described as a chilling scream.

In the summer of 1977, several people stood on a hill in the Elizabeth Lake area and watched three Bigfoot playing in a meadow below, and about a month later, eight hikers in the Cuberant Basin watched what they described as an eight-foot tall white creature.

Many of these accounts made it into the local papers, including the one where Lee Fielding, an employee of Utah Wildlife Resources, was camped near Elizabeth Mountain when something came into his camp, frightening his horses away. The next morning, he met some hunters leaving the area, scared by what they described as a Bigfoot.

Other Uinta accounts include people hearing whoops, screams, and howls, a man being chased on his dirt bike in the Francis Peak region, Ute Indians seeing Bigfoot in a canyon on their reservation (which the Uintas bisect), and a man and his son finding huge tracks in their logging camp.

And that was just the 1970s and 80s. Bigfoot's been sighted many times in the Uintas since then, by Boy Scout troops and teachers and forest rangers. Of all Utah's wild country, the Uintas are possibly the region best suited to Bigfoot in terms of habitat.

Before too long, I was in Evanston, Wyoming, and had made my decision—I would go up onto the North Slope of the Uintas and camp near Elizabeth Lake. The North Slope saw fewer people, and I'd always wanted to go visit that area, as it seemed like many of the Bigfoot sightings had come from there.

I stopped and bought a few supplies, then continued south, soon passing back into Utah. After gradually climbing from high desert to forest, I soon came to the Bear Creek Lodge, a row of log cabins with a sign offering ATVs for rent. The highway was now traversing a thick aspen and pine forest, and I could make out one of the high peaks of the Uintas far ahead, still covered with snow, even this late in the summer.

According to my map, there was a road just past the lodge called Elizabeth Mountain Road that went fairly close to Elizabeth Lake.

After passing the lodge, I immediately came to a sign that said, "Wasatch National Forest, Land of Many Uses," and I turned onto a wide road that looked to be well maintained, but with no signage. A number of side roads branched off that looked like ATV trails. I saw nary a soul as the road continued slowly climbing up into the forest.

After a few miles, I came upon an old pioneer log cabin slowly sinking into the wet grasses of one of the most beautiful meadows I'd ever seen. The roof was long gone, and the wood so weathered it had turned gray. Wildflowers were everywhere, and I had a sudden feeling that I was home.

I stopped and got out. Everything seemed so quiet, so peaceful, and I walked around the cabin, wondering who had built it and what had become of them. Why build in a place that was sure to be under many feet of snow in the winter? It had to be for summer use only.

My map said I was in the McKenzie Creek area—the creek had to be named after someone named McKenzie, and had he also built the cabin? Was he a logger? Had he come from Scotland to make a better life in America? Did he like these Uinta highlands as much as the Highlands in Scotland?

One wall of the cabin had fallen partially down where the logs had rotted apart, exposed to the weather because of the missing roof. I managed to climb up the wall, using the logs for steps, and went on into the small building—and that's when I saw it.

There was grass growing inside the cabin in the dirt floor that was partially matted down into a large circle, much like the bed of some large animal.

I stood there for a minute, wondering what could have made it, first thinking of moose—but the cabin would be impossible for anything with four legs to enter. I'd had to scramble a bit myself to scale the wall.

Now the silence seemed to take on an almost ominous feel. I knew I was in Bigfoot country—had I stumbled upon a Bigfoot nest? Getting into the cabin would be easy for a Bigfoot, and it would make a cozy place to sleep. Nothing could get in to bother the Big Guy, though you'd have to be crazy to want to bother him, especially when he was sleeping.

I examined the nest a little closer, hoping to find a clump of hair or anything that I could take home to examine closer. But I found nothing—except when I bent down close to the flattened grasses, I could smell a faint odor like a skunk.

Had a skunk climbed the wall and holed up here? It seemed pretty unlikely, unless skunks are good at climbing. How about a bear? It was possible, but I'd never heard of bears smelling like skunks, but maybe they did sometimes.

I climbed back out, then wandered around the old cabin a bit, looking for tracks or for some hint at what had made the nest.

It was then that I saw it—something dark and tall stood at the edge of the meadow, partially hidden in the shade of the trees, watching me.

12. The Blacks Fork River

· ·

I felt a chill go through me. I didn't want to let on that I was afraid, so I turned and began slowly walking back to my pickup, acting as if I hadn't seen it. I tried to be nonchalant, but my heart was racing a mile a minute.

Finally, after what seemed like forever, I reached my truck and got inside. I had been afraid to look back, but as I started up the engine, I looked in the direction of the figure.

It was gone.

It must've stepped back into the trees where I could no longer see it, or maybe it had left completely. I didn't want to know which, I just wanted to leave.

I backed around and took off on the road, continuing on uphill, even though I wanted to turn and go back the way I'd come. I'd wanted to camp in the Uintas for years, and I wasn't going to let some shadowy figure stop me at this point.

The road immediately curved to the right, and as I followed it, I saw someone on an ATV riding from the direction of the back side of the cabin.

I felt a sense of relief. That had to be the figure I saw looking at me from the edge of the forest. Probably someone checking the cabin out, just like I had been. I soon saw them in my rearview mirror, going the other direction. Must be someone who rented an ATV from the lodge, I figured.

As I drove on, slowly gaining elevation, I wondered why I'd felt such a sense of peacefulness at the cabin. It was almost as if I'd been there before, as if it had once been home. I knew that wasn't possible, but it must have triggered some good association at a subconscious level for me to feel that way.

Maybe I'd had something good happen at a similar cabin and was generalizing, though I wasn't sure what it could be. But I'd been raised in similar country, so maybe my parents had taken me on a nice picnic at a cabin or something.

I was now on the North Slope of the Uintas, and the views were getting more and more spectacular, the high rugged peaks draped with huge fields of snow, surprising for this late in the summer.

I soon came to a lake that the map called Fish Lake and thought about camping there, then decided to keep going, as it was too close to the road. The sun was now hanging low in the sky, and I needed to find a place soon. But for some reason that dark figure back by the cabin made me want to get farther away, so I kept driving.

I soon came to sign that said:

"North Slope Road, Elizabeth Ridge, Elevation 10,235."

Below that, pointing one way, "Green River Drainage, Blacks Forks River," and pointing the other, "Great Basin Drainage, Bear River."

I could feel the altitude a little, but it surprised me to see I was that high up. I'd climbed so gradually that it didn't feel like it at all.

Not long after, I came to a crossroads. I was at the West Fork of the Blacks Fork River, according to the map, and I could see the curves of the river gently meandering down a beautiful wide valley. Being a fly-fisherman, I knew I had to go check it out—I had no choice. The fish were calling me.

I turned onto a narrow dirt road that followed the sinuous curves of the river, and I soon stopped at a small meadow—this would be a perfect place to camp. I could put my tent right by my pickup, and there was even a fire ring already there, evidence that I wasn't the first to like the spot. If I hurried, I could do a little fishing before sunset and maybe even have a nice trout dinner.

I conveniently forgot I didn't have a Utah license, something I would never condone in one of my clients, but I was enthralled with this little stream in one of the most picturesque valleys I'd ever seen, and civilization and its trappings (including fishing licenses) seemed far away.

I guess I figured if a wildlife officer came by, I could always say I thought I was still in Wyoming and hope he didn't ask to see my Wyoming license. But it was late enough in the day I didn't figure I'd see anyone. I found out later I was wrong, but it was much later, and it wasn't a game and fish officer.

Since I was fishing a small stream, I decided a Wooly Bugger lure would mimic an aquatic insect and attract those nice rainbow trout that I knew had to be lurking in the shadows. I had a beautiful red and black Wooly Bugger with a gold spinner that would be just right. In late summer, the trout are harder to find, and a spinner between the fly and the leader causes disturbances in the water that catches the trout's attention.

I won't get into the lore of the fishing lure, or maybe I should say the lure of fishing, but let me just say that when I'm fishing, time stops. It was almost dark by the time I caught my first trout, which I released, as it was too small.

Finally, I kind of woke up from my fishing trance and looked around me, noting it was evening. Where had the time gone? I quickly realized that I still needed to set up my tent, but by the time I'd put away my fishing gear and watched a blazing red sunset, it was getting really dark.

So, I once again opted to sleep in the back of my truck, under the security of my new-to-me topper. It was just so easy—throw in my pad and bag and crawl in. No need to worry about rain or bears—or Bigfoot—or so I hoped, anyway.

Before I crawled in, I stood a bit and looked at the stars, which were so thick I could barely make out any familiar constellations. Everything blended together in a mass of white and silver and gold and red twinkles. It was stunningly beautiful, and I again felt that same sense of being home that I'd felt at the cabin.

Had my parents brought me here when I was too young to remember it? I would probably never know, but there was something about this place that felt comfortable and homey. Even though I knew I was probably the only human for many square miles of wild forest, I felt like I belonged here, like it was the home of coyotes and rabbits and black bears, but also mine.

I ate some crackers and cheese, washed it all down with some water, then crawled into my bag and lay there for awhile, just savoring the feeling of security. Strange, to feel like this out in the middle of nowhere, I thought, thinking back to how afraid I'd been everywhere else on my expedition.

I soon drifted off into a deep refreshing sleep, so refreshing that when I woke, I thought it should be morning and was surprised to see it was only four a.m.

I slipped out of the truck to go take a pee. The half-moon lit up the meadow around me, the river looking like a black ribbon cutting through the soft silver grasses.

I was about to climb back into the truck when I saw movement up on the road above me. I froze.

I soon saw two tall—and I mean tall, as in seven-feet tall—figures walking down the road at a slow but steady pace. I knew they could see my white truck below them in the moonlight. I wasn't really afraid, but I hoped they wouldn't see me, my back pressed against the pickup.

They walked slowly, with purpose, never once turning to look at me, and were soon gone. It was strange enough that they were so tall and were walking so slowly in the moonlight out in the middle of nowhere, but what was really puzzling was the fact that they looked like they were wearing long monk's robes.

I crawled into the front of my pickup and locked the doors and waited for dawn.

13. Quiet Days in the High Country

When I woke, I was in the back of my truck in my sleeping bag. It was about seven a.m., and I wondered how I'd gotten into the back again. I must've drifted back to sleep, then woke up and crawled under the topper in a semi-comatose state—why else couldn't I recall it?

I got up and started making coffee over my little Coleman stove, trying to wake up. I had a feeling in the back of my mind that something was off.

You know how you first wake up and feel that something's different, but you aren't sure what it is? Then you suddenly remember that it's the day of something big or maybe something major happened the day before—but there's that moment when your memory hasn't kicked in, yet you know something's off.

Well, that's how I felt—and then I remembered the two figures. I knew I'd seen them, yet I wasn't a bit afraid—I still felt that same peaceful feeling I'd had before.

I grabbed my coffee mug and walked up to the road, looking for tracks where the pair had walked. There was nothing, but the dirt was hard packed and not conducive to track-making. I wasn't even leaving tracks as I walked along, so I didn't really expect to find anything.

Had the pair been bears? Did bears stroll along roads in pairs in the moonlight? Were they out on a date? I laughed at myself—it just didn't seem like they could've been bears.

Occam's Razor says the simplest explanation is usually the correct one, and the simplest explanation was that two really tall monks were walking down a back road in the Uinta Mountains in the middle of the night. Well, that seemed simpler than saying it was a pair of bears in monk's robes, anyway.

OK, they were monks. I would just accept it and be on my way. Maybe there was a secret monastery nearby and the monks liked to go out in the moonlight and walk around in the wee hours of the morn.

But somehow that explanation didn't sit right. I'd heard that the High Uintas were home to high strangeness—though actually being there, it just seemed like any other impressive mountain range, except maybe less frequented by people.

I thought again of Occam's Razor. The simplest explanation was really that it had all been a dream. I tried to lean back against my truck just like I had when watching the pair, and I then realized that a bush next to it made it impossible. It had to have been a dream, though it would've been the most realistic dream I'd ever had.

Now what? For some reason, the desire to fish was completely gone, replaced by a desire to explore. I was really enjoying my time here, in spite of the strangeness of the previous night, and I wanted to go even deeper into these enchanted-feeling mountains.

The map showed the little road I was on petering out in a few miles, so after a quick breakfast of canned peaches and a granola bar, I got into my truck and turned around, getting back onto the main road again. It was a beautiful sunny day, with white clouds floating across a deep blue sky, what we called a bluebird sky back in Colorado.

Utah's Uinta Mountains were no longer as primitive as they'd been back in the 1970s when the first Bigfoot accounts came from there, as they were getting more and more discovered, not only for recreation but also by the mineral and gas industry. But they were still pretty far off the beaten track, and one could still hike into the backcountry and not see another human for weeks, which was my kind of country—and also Bigfoot country, I suspected.

The range had the rare distinction of running east-west, which, to my knowledge, can be said of only one other major range in the U.S.—the Brooks Range in Alaska. Sarah told me earlier that geologists thought maybe the Uintas had once been an island accretion, a group of islands stuck millions of years ago by tectonic forces to what was at that time the North American landmass, and thus the east-west direction.

In any case, they were one of the most unique and ethereal ranges I'd ever been in, with their dense pine and aspen forests that framed towering granite peaks like jewels. The range actually stretched from near Salt Lake City into the northwestern corner of Colorado, a distance of about 120 miles, with Kings Peak the highest point at 13,528 feet.

Anyway, I loved it there and wanted to stay, so I spent the next three days wandering around on backroads, lost half the time, finally getting up the courage to sleep outside under some of the clearest skies I'd ever seen. And the whole time, that sense of peacefulness never left me.

I decided not to test my luck by fishing without a license, even if I did release, and instead spent my time taking hikes through the thick forests, daydreaming, playing my guitar, and half-hoping I would see a Bigfoot, but not too disappointed when I didn't. I even tried a few whoops at one point, but got no response.

The only thing of note that happened was the last evening there when I saw two figures jogging towards me through the meadow I was camped in. I was instantly on full alert, as they were the first people I'd seen the whole time, and I wasn't sure why they would be running. But they turned out to be adventure runners trying to break their own record for traversing the Highline Trail, which is the highest continuous trail in the Uintas and runs 100 miles.

They had started at dawn that same day and were trying to get to the end of a 70-mile stretch of the trail by dawn the next day. They already held the record for that stretch, having run it in 29 hours the year before. Much of the trail is above 10,000 feet, and they also would summit a number of passes, some almost 13,000-feet high.

They stopped and asked for water, and I refilled their bottles from my containers, then offered them some granola bars, but they instead took a short break and ate tacos they'd got from Taco Bell in Roosevelt, the town on the other end of the Uintas where they'd started. They told me they'd each had ten tacos so far, as well as numerous granola bars and gorp. They did eat some of my canned peaches, which they said would give them quick energy.

I didn't envy them trying to wayfind in the dark, but they told me they had a GPS that would keep them on the trail. It seems like the previous year they'd lost about four hours to being off-trail, so they were more prepared this time and confident they could break their old record.

In all honesty, they looked pretty ragged, and I questioned their ability to run through the entire night, especially at altitude, but they seemed not only ready, but eager to get going. I sure didn't envy them any and wondered how it must feel to be so motivated.

About the only time I felt that motivated was when I had a big rainbow on the hook and wanted to pull it in, and that was what some would call a mindless short-term motivation.

We talked while they ate, and as they prepared to depart, I had a final question for them.

"You guys see anything out there that might remind you of Bigfoot?"

One guy, Kerry, grinned, but the other, Craig, turned kind of pale.

Craig replied, "Last time we were out here, it was about four in the morning when someone started running next to me on the trail. I thought it was Kerry and said something to him, but he never responded, and then all of a sudden I realized he was ahead of me, as I could see his flashlight. I hoofed it and caught up to him, and we stuck together after that. I don't know what it was, but it was running on two feet, and it scared the crap out of me."

Kerry added, "I had hoped to forget about that, but thanks for the reminder. We need to stick together tonight." He gave Craig a knowing look.

They settled their daypacks onto their shoulders, then bade me farewell and took off running down the trail.

I wanted to ask if the figure had been wearing a monk's robe, but they were gone.

14. More High Strangeness

That night, I decided to sleep in the pickup bed again, probably because of what the pair had told me about their mysterious running companion.

I had dawdled too long and needed to get back on the Bigfoot trail, though if Bigfoot weren't in the Uintas, I doubted I would find him anywhere. I decided to head out the next morning for Montana. Like I mentioned earlier, I had a rendezvous up there, though it wasn't one I was particularly looking forward to.

For some reason, as I lay there in my sleeping bag, missing Sarah, I started thinking of a story I'd read once about a guy who spent a lot of time in the Uintas as a kid.

He had lots of strange stories to tell, but in this particular one, he and a friend were in their late teens and were spending a winter weekend in the family camp trailer near Strawberry Reservoir, a popular fishing lake southwest of the Uintas. The pair was up there for the weekend, rabbit hunting and ice fishing, as they often did. It was 1978.

One night, they were inside when they heard a strange booming sound, and thinking it was a storm coming in, they stepped out to take a look, wondering if they might need to leave. But the sky was clear and cold, and the booming seemed to be coming from beneath the ice in the large lake, which seemed odd, but they figured maybe it was ice breaking up from pressure from the deep ice cover.

They went back inside and slept soundly until about two a.m., when they heard a boom that was so loud it seemed to cut through them. They grabbed their rifles and ran outside just in time to hear a strange whooshing sound that seemed to be following the shoreline.

As it came nearer, they ran back inside and watched out a window as a huge wave broke through the ice along the shore and pushed water a good 10 feet from the lake, continuing on around the shoreline.

Shocked, they tried to figure out what was going on. The lake surface continued to rock a bit, then settled down, so they decided it must have been an earthquake. But shortly after, they could see a strange light under the ice, moving along the shoreline, and which then sped up and disappeared.

Of course, they were now terrified, and after staying up all night, opted to leave the next morning.

That same guy also wrote of going out one night in his pickup and being trapped by tree fall up on Strawberry Ridge and seeing a large dark figure in the night that they knew was a Bigfoot. The guy and his friend were armed and managed to wait out the night, then drove around one of the freshly-felled trees the next morning. They actually heard the trees fall and knew it was a trap.

As I lay there, I wondered about his stories and if they were true. Some of them seemed kind of far-fetched, and

I thought again about what I'd read at the Utah State University library about folklore. I knew that the 1950s and 60s were a time for many UFO sightings and stories, and I also knew that this strangeness continued somewhat into the 1970s, along with other odd tales.

Could it all be a part of the culture of that time, of people having a heightened awareness of strange things, an awareness that might have been created by Cold War fears, along with shows like the "Twilight Zone"?

I knew that in my own part of the country, in Washington state, as well as northwest Colorado and all over the country, there had been lots of strange tales told during that same era. Or was it just that lots of strange things actually happened during that period?

I didn't know the answer, but I still believed that Bigfoot was a mammal just like myself, and I had a hard time believing stories that painted him or her elsewise, as many of these strange tales did, adding a UFO component or such.

I personally knew that living on the edge of wild country could easily spawn strange tales, especially if one didn't feel comfortable with wilderness. Were such tales like those tales of boogeymen told to try and keep us from going into areas we were uncertain about, places where we might be harmed? It did seem to me that, as civilization pushed deeper into such wild areas, the stories seemed to decrease. Education and awareness seemed pretty effective ways to push out superstition and fear.

I had to again ask myself if my fears were superstition, or was it actually possible Bigfoot could exist? At this point, I didn't feel qualified to answer any questions, especially those concerning my own beliefs, as I was too close to the subject matter to be objective.

As I lay there, I thought I could imagine the strange booming sound that the storyteller had heard that deep winter's night near Strawberry Reservoir. The longer I listened, the more that sense of peace I'd felt for the past few days seemed to dissipate, and the more fearful I became, as the booms moved closer and became louder.

Finally, a bolt of lightning sounded like it hit the ridge above my camp, shaking me from imagination back into reality. A thunderstorm had moved in, following the mares' tails I'd noticed earlier in the day, precursor to summer storms.

I felt kind of silly, the smell of ozone permeating the night air, confirming that the bolt had been close. What had I been thinking, that the booming was something out of the norm when it was just a storm? The power of the human imagination struck me, just like that bolt had hit the ridge.

But now I wondered how safe I was. Should I get into the cab of the truck? Was I safer there?

I jumped out and into the cab just as the pitter patter of rain began on the truck's metal roof. Another bolt struck nearby, lighting up the meadow around me in an eerie blue glow and making me instinctively duck.

The storm moved through quickly, leaving the now three-quarters moon draped with misty clouds and muting its light into an almost ghostly gray. Soon the rain stopped, and I crawled back under the topper and was soon fast asleep to the sounds of distant booms as the storm moved on.

I woke in the morning to a strange sound, one I'd not heard often—the sound of bleating and bells amidst someone yelling in Spanish something that sounded like, "Alto ah, alto ah, alto aqui!"

I suspected I was smack in the middle of a herd of sheep, and one look at a white sea out the back window confirmed my suspicion.

15. Osos

. . . .

It didn't take long for the herd to settle down and start grazing, which meant I could finally get out of my truck without worrying about being stampeded.

My camp chair was knocked over and stepped on a dozen times, from the looks of it. Everything else was in my truck, fortunately.

As I stood looking at my trampled chair, a short and slight man walked up, holding the reins of a rangy bay Quarter horse and followed by a handsome stock dog. The man appeared to be Mexican, which I affirmed though my brilliant use of Spanish.

"Como estas?" I said.

"Bien, gracious," he replied, then started speaking Spanish so fast I was immediately lost. Of course, I would've been just as lost if he'd spoken it slowly, since I know very little of the language. My simple question must have made him think I knew more than I did.

"No habla Espanol," I said. "Lo siento."

That was about all I could say—"I don't speak Spanish, sorry."

He nodded his head a bit sorrowfully. I couldn't imagine what it must be like to go through much of your life far from home and family with nobody ever understanding a word you were saying.

I had guessed he was from Mexico, as the majority of sheepherders in Utah and Colorado were either Mexican or Basque. They worked hard and sent much of their small salaries to their families, though the Basques typically were by now American citizens and spoke good English, descendants of earlier immigrant sheepherders.

"Estoy Ricardo," the sheepherder said.

"Estoy Rusty," I replied. We shook hands. At least we shared that one cultural form of greeting.

I wasn't sure what to say at that point, as I knew he probably spoke very little English, if any, but I tried anyway.

"Do you speak English?"

"No," he replied, even more sorrowfully. He then added, "Tiene cigarette?"

Well, I thought, at least he knew the important stuff.

"Lo siento," I answered.

"Azucar? Sugar?" He didn't give up easily.

I went to the cab of my truck and rummaged through my food box on the floor. I kept it in the front to help reduce food smells, not wanting to attract bears. Of course, I knew a bear could rip the door off my cab if it wanted, but I hoped the bears in these parts weren't that bold or savvy.

I returned with a box of granola bars, some chocolate bars, and some apples, and handed them to him.

His face brightened. "Muchas gracious," he thanked me.

"It's bien," I replied.

As he opened a granola bar, it occurred to me that I was looking at someone who spent months in this country all alone, totally solitary except for his sheep, dog, and horse, dealing with whatever nature handed him, totally solo.

I suddenly felt humbled. Here I was, half afraid to even sleep outside, and this man thought nothing of living his life out here, far from any kind of civilization, except when his employer brought him supplies. He not only lived alone in the wilds, he didn't even have a vehicle. All he had was a sheep wagon for protection, though the ones I'd seen seemed more than adequate, for bad weather, anyway. I wasn't so sure about bears.

I was now curious as to what kind of animals he'd encountered, as I knew he covered way more territory with his sheep than the average hiker or horsepacker in the Uintas. If there were Bigfoot up here, he had probably seen or heard one. But how could I ask him, when I didn't speak Spanish and he didn't know English?

I picked up a stick and drew a Bigfoot print in the dirt, then asked, "You ever see this?"

I spoke really slowly, hoping he would understand.

He shook his head in puzzlement.

"Nunca. Que es?"

"Bigfoot," I replied. "Grande foot."

"Oso?" he asked.

"No, no oso, no bear, Bigfoot," I answered.

I then drew a sketch of a Bigfoot in the dirt.

He looked closely at the sketch, then at me, then back at the sketch. I watched his face closely, as I knew he might not wish to share any Bigfoot sightings he may have had with a complete stranger.

"Nunca," he said. "Adios, y gracious."

He then quickly mounted his horse, riding off, his dog at the horse's heels. Before I could say sickem, he was gone, clear around on the other side of the big herd, far across the meadow.

I was a bit stunned. Whatever he'd been thinking, it had to have bothered him for him to just ride off like that. Why would he have that reaction? Had he seen Bigfoot and wanted nothing to do with it or anyone who mentioned it? Was he superstitious about it, thinking maybe it was something evil, and thereby so was I for talking about it?

I had no idea, but I knew it was a dead end. I would never know what he was thinking or what he'd seen, if anything. It was time to concede my beautiful meadow to the four-footed locusts and head out.

I climbed into my pickup and turned back down the road. I had to go to Montana, and this whole Uinta trip had been a giant sidetrack, as enjoyable as it had been. I'd run into my share of mysteries here, and I'd thoroughly enjoyed the magnificent mountains, but the mystery of Bigfoot was no closer to a solution for me.

I had one last place I wanted to visit before heading north, and it wasn't all that far away at this point, just over on the east side of the Uintas in the Uinta Basin, near

Roosevelt, Utah. I could be there in less than two hours. In fact, if I just kept going, I could be home in less than four hours.

The thought was tempting, but I knew I needed to carry on with my quest. I might never have another opportunity, with work and bills and winter coming on sooner than I wanted. And Sarah was encouraging me to stay out, as she knew it was something I'd been wanting to do for years—or maybe she was enjoying her solitude, I thought wryly. But next time, she might not be so encouraging.

I called Sarah to let her know where I was, but I conveniently neglected to tell her where I was going, as I didn't want to worry her. Her voice was comforting, and I knew I would need all the comfort I could get, given my destination.

My next stop would be the infamous Skinwalker Ranch.

16. Skinwalker Ranch

I had been slowly working my way east during the past few days, so the Skinwalker Ranch, which was in the Uinta Basin just below the eastern flanks of the Uinta Mountains, southeast of the small town of Roosevelt, wasn't all that far.

As I drove along, I thought of all the strange tales I'd heard about the ranch, and I also wondered at yet another sidetrack—this one into what was clearly the paranormal, something I really didn't put that much credence in.

But there had supposedly been Bigfoot sighted on the ranch, along with aliens and weird spacecraft and lights and whatnot, and I wanted to find out if Bigfoot really did hobnob with aliens, as some seemed to think.

I had no idea how I was going to determine whether Bigfoot was at the ranch or not, but to go see a place that was so notorious, especially since it was so close, just seemed logical—well, in an illogical sort of way, if you consider the superstitious nature of the whole thing.

I'd never seen a ghost, UFO, skinwalker, wolfman—well, you get the picture—and I was well acquainted with the human propensity for imagining and mistaking things—I'd done it myself more than once. So I admit to being pretty skeptical about the ranch, but I wanted to go see it anyway. I will admit that later my skepticism waned somewhat during the darkness of night.

The Skinwalker Ranch was once called the Sherman (or Gorman) Ranch after its owners, a couple who purchased the 480-acre property in 1994. Soon after moving onto the ranch, the Shermans supposedly began to witness strange happenings. A reporter got wind of the events and began writing about them, creating instant notoriety for the ranch.

The family eventually fled, selling the ranch to its current owner, Robert Bigelow, a wealthy entrepreneur who purchased it in 1996. Bigelow then installed a group of scientists at the ranch to observe and report back on the weird activities.

After a book called "Hunt for the Skinwalker" was written about the ranch by the same reporter, it began to be called the Skinwalker Ranch, and a movie by that name added to the notoriety about the supposed strangeness there. That was about all I knew about it, except that Bigfoot had supposedly been sighted there. I hadn't read the book.

I continued east, and upon reaching the Uinta Basin, I stopped in the small town of Roosevelt, which reminded me of towns in my home area of northwest Colorado, now only a hundred or so miles away. I was near the Northern Ute Reservation. After getting gas and groceries, I sat down on a bench outside the grocery store and people-watched while eating an ice-cream cone, the first I'd had in ages.

I was kind of hoping someone would be friendly enough for me to ask some questions about the ranch, though I had a suspicion these seemingly pragmatic Westerners wouldn't think too highly of strangers invading their town in the hopes of seeing aliens.

Before long, a man who looked to be an old-timer stopped and asked me how I was doing. He had that look that one acquires from spending a lot of time outdoors, making his skin tan and wrinkled, and he wore the classic uniform of old-time Westerners—Levis, a plaid long-sleeved shirt with the sleeves rolled up, a faded felt cowboy hat, and old run-down ranch boots. He looked like the kind of guy who could tell a few good tales or two.

"Howdy," he greeted me, stopping.

"Hi," I replied, motioning for him to sit down by me. I suspected he was bored, as many older folks tend to be, having lots of free time. Maybe he could tell me about the ranch. He sat down. I was once again struck by the friendliness of these folk.

"What's a fine-looking young man like yourself doing in backwater Roosevelt, Utah, if you don't mind me askin'?" He held out his hand, adding, "I'm Jim. Used to own the biggest ranch in the Uinta Basin, which ain't sayin' much, cause most of the land belongs to the Utes."

He had a twinkle in his eye, and I immediately liked him.

I answered, "I'm Rusty. I'm a fishing guide from over in Colorado. I've been camping up in the mountains, but now I want to go to the Skinwalker Ranch, but I'm not sure exactly where it is."

He sat there, grinning at me like he knew some secret I didn't and that he wasn't going to tell.

Finally, he said, "Why in hellsbells do ya wanna go out there for? Ain't nothin' there worth lookin' at. Sure as hell ain't none of them skinwalkers. They's Navajo, and this is Ute country. Utes have stickmen, not skinwalkers, but there ain't none of them out there, neither. And some of us call it the Bigelow Ranch."

I wasn't sure how to answer, but I finally said, "I don't know. I'm just curious. I heard there were Bigfoot sighted out there, and I'm interested in Bigfoot, I guess." It all suddenly sounded kind of lame to me.

Jim continued grinning as he pulled a can of tobacco from his shirt pocket and started rolling a cigarette.

"There's everything out there, if you believe the stories—flying saucers, black triangles, bulletproof wolves, poltergeist, Bigfoot, alien portals, invisible things attacking horses and cattle, floating orbs of light, and worst of all, supposed scientists! It's enough to keep an honest man awake at night."

I laughed. "Sounds like you're a skeptic."

"Nah, I just know some of the neighbors. Ain't nuthin' out there except coyotes and jackrabbits—and a few cattle. And last I heard even the scientists left. Only guy out there's the caretaker, and if he ever sees anything it's in the bottom of a bottle."

"You're saying the neighbors don't believe any of it either?"

"Nah, it was just a hoax. Great way to unload a worthless bunch of sagebrush. And it worked."

"So, there aren't any Bigfoot?"

Jim paused, inhaling cigarette smoke, then stood and exhaled as he talked.

"No Bigfoot. If you want Bigfoot, you have to go up there." He jerked his thumb back over his shoulder towards the distant Uinta Mountains, then added, "I ain't never seen one, but unlike the stuff over at the Bigelow Ranch, I think they just might be real. One of my old buddies, Rich Seeley, he runs sheep, and he has a heckuvva time keeping sheepherders, if you know what I mean."

"Does anyone around here talk about Bigfoot much? I mean, does anyone ever see them?"

"Besides sheepherders? Not really, not that I know of, anyway. Once in awhile some Ute will talk about one up in some canyon on the rez, but usually it's way over in the Bookcliffs. No way to verify nuthin' cause it's off limits if you ain't Ute. Me, like I said, I ain't never seen one. But they're a lot more probable than the stuff out at Bigelow's place."

Jim paused, then added, "Young man, if you wanna go out to the Bigelow Ranch, you just stay on 40 going east, then turn south on past Ft. Duchesne, then when you get to 2750 South, you hang a right. Go on up the road a ways and you'll see the locked gate. The road dead ends there. There's a shorter way on out by Ballard, but this way's the easiest. But take my word for it, you'll wanna get outta there before dark."

"Why is that?" I ask, puzzled, since he'd said there was nothing going on.

"Because the tribal lawmen keep an eye out and might harass you. They're gettin' tired of the fruits and nuts comin' around, no offense, since you don't seem like one. But I gotta run. You know, I used to fish a lot, but my wife won't let me go very far from home now, with my old ticker only half tickin'."

I laughed. "I'm mostly on vacation from fishing right now. Just camping out."

"Well," Jim replied. "I hope you like your stay here. I sure enjoyed talkin' to you. I'm not sure whether to wish you good luck or not in seeing a Bigfoot."

With that, Jim tossed his cigarette butt onto the ground and stomped on it and went on into the store.

I got into my pickup and headed east on Highway 40, just like he'd told me to, then turned south after a few miles.

If I'd blinked, I wouldn't have noticed the tiny town of Fort Duchesne, headquarters of the Northern Utes, though I did notice a sign that pointed west to Bottle Hollow Reservoir. I could see the small dam from the edge of town.

Continuing south, the landscape was high desert scrub, with sagebrush and creosote, dotted here and there with a hayfield or ranch house.

I soon came to the road where Jim had said to turn and found myself between a mesa and more hayfields. I passed several houses and a small ranch, then the road ended at a locked gate with a sign that said, "Keep Out." Behind the gate down the lane a ways stood an old farmhouse and corrals and various ranch equipment. And that was all.

I sat there for a minute, then turned around and left. I was sure I wasn't the first to seek out the Skinwalker Ranch and feel disappointed. There was nothing about it that indicated anything unusual, not even a sign that said, "Skinwalker Ranch." It was just a small ranch, like many others all over the country. I felt a bit sheepish, like I'd let the hype fool me.

As I turned back north, I realized it was getting dark and I had no idea where I was going to camp. From the looks of things, everything was either Ute Reservation land or private. I decided to go back to Bottle Hollow Reservoir, as it sounded somewhat promising. Maybe there were some camp spots there.

As I reached the reservoir, I could tell I was now on the backside of the Skinwalker Ranch, nothing between me and it except for the big mesa where all the weird things supposedly took place.

It might make for an interesting night, I thought, as I circled the lake and came to a recreation area and boat ramp. There were a number of developed camp sites, each with a picnic table. A couple of camp trailers were parked in sites, but nobody was around, and I knew I could just pull into one of the spots and sleep in my pickup.

Since I wasn't at Skinwalker Ranch, I didn't expect anything unusual. I would soon be proved wrong.

17. Bottle Hollow Lights

. . . .

I later read up some on Bottle Hollow Reservoir and found it had once been a resort with a motel and convention center, all built on reservation land. This was back in the 1970s, before a lot of tribes realized the income potential from tourism and casinos, so Bottle Hollow was ahead of its time. There had been a dinner theater there, as well as conventions and even fashion shows around a big swimming pool.

The reservoir got its name from Bottle Hollow, a ravine that was once full of old bottles tossed there by drunk soldiers returning to Fort Duchesne in the late 1800s. That ravine was now underwater.

What I didn't know when camped there that night was that, like Bear Lake, Bottle Hollow Reservoir supposedly had a monster in its depths. The Utes had stories about a large snake that would come out of the waters and crawl around the shoreline, apparently looking for people to grab and drag back down into the lake.

In one such story, a couple was swimming at night when the woman was grabbed and dragged under. The man swam underwater to save her, where he saw a huge black snake. He was able to rescue the woman, but she died anyway from trauma.

Others say the reservoir sees an inordinately high number of drownings, and yet others have observed strange lights going in and out of the water.

At that time, I had no inkling about any of this and just parked my truck, made myself a sandwich for dinner, then sat on the tailgate and played my guitar. I was more interested in the goings-on at the Skinwalker Ranch just to the south of me than anything at the reservoir, and as night fell, I couldn't help but keep searching the sky over the ranch for weird lights.

It's funny how the most hardcore skeptic can become less skeptical when alone out in the dark, especially in wild country. I believe it's just hardwired into us, probably as a survival mechanism. We can disavow any belief of strange things by day, but at night, well, we may still not believe, but let's just say the door of uncertainty has been pushed open a crack by some mysterious force. That force may be our own imaginations, but it can seem very real.

Anyway, as I sat there, playing my guitar, the moon rose over the distant hills and reflected off the lake waters, making everything seem very mysterious, and I began to feel a sense of unease. There were now lights in the two camp trailers, but I'd parked as far from them as I could, at the other end of the campground.

As I mentioned, I knew nothing about Bottle Hollow Reservoir at that time, and very little about Skinwalker Ranch. I just knew the ranch was supposedly the site of paranormal activity, but I wasn't sure exactly what kind.

As I set there, the waters began to shimmer, and the nearly-full moon lit up a few wispy clouds overhead. It was actually really beautiful, and I stopped playing my guitar and just sat there, watching the somewhat surreal scene of moonlit waters stretched out before me. I had no idea how deep the reservoir was, but it seemed really deep.

I once again thought of my search for Bigfoot and wondered if it weren't a fool's quest. Thinking back on how sketchy I'd felt since starting out, it did at least seem like I'd finally conquered my fears. The strange undefinable feelings I'd kept having after dark, the fears of the unknown, seemed to have abated. After a few peaceful nights in the Uintas, I was feeling more like I used to, enjoying the solitude and peace of the outdoors.

Ironically, it was while I was thinking about how I'd conquered my fears that I saw something like I'd never seen, something that scared the bejeebers out of me.

There, right over Skinwalker Ranch, I could suddenly see a group of strange lights that seemed to bob and sway, be stationary for awhile, then move again. I at first thought they had to be some kind of planes in formation, probably military, in the distance, and they would soon be overhead, as they appeared to be coming my direction.

But they then appeared to stop and just hang in the sky. I quickly grabbed my binoculars from the front seat of my truck, knowing the lights would eventually disappear if they were planes. But when I turned again to look, they were still there. I was able to steady my binoculars enough to zoom in by leaning against the hood of my truck. I realized they were too low in the sky to be planes.

There were six fuzzy orbs of light just hanging in the air, and they appeared to be about a mile away, exactly over Skinwalker Ranch. I held my breath in suspense, wondering if I were witnessing my first UFOs. Well, technically, I knew I was, as I sure couldn't identify them, whether they were of extraterrestrial origin or not.

As I watched, they dissipated, much like a gas lantern when put out—the lights kind of dimmed, then flickered, then were gone.

I sat for some time, watching in disbelief, wondering if I'd really seen anything at all. Was it some kind of hysteria? Was I primed to see something strange and had thus created a self-fulfilling prophecy, my brain helping fulfill it through hallucination?

Try as I might, I couldn't shake the feeling that what I'd seen was real, not a product of my brain. The lights were stationary and I'd even walked around a bit, trying to view them at a different angle with my binoculars, plus they acted like a real object, not changing size or anything like that.

I thought of swamp gas and ball lightning as explanations, but the sky was clear and the lights were over arid desert.

I now put my guitar away. I couldn't shake the strange feeling, try as I may. I was pretty sure I wouldn't be able to sleep. I kept looking towards the ranch, expecting to see more lights, but there was nothing.

I wanted to talk to Sarah for reassurance, but even though it was only about 10 p.m., it was too late to call her. She was working a summer job, doing research for an oil company, and I knew she had to get up early every day to get out to the field.

In fact, her job was what had freed me financially from having to work as a guide for a couple of months, and I sure didn't want to interfere with her sleep—and I knew strange tales of lights in the sky over Skinwalker Ranch would bother her. She would probably demand I leave immediately, then be up half the night worrying about me.

As a breeze stirred the waters of the reservoir, I decided to leave. I just wasn't into strange things, which some would find ironic, knowing of my interest in Bigfoot.

But to me, Bigfoot is a real flesh-and-blood creature, a mammal, just like I am. Tales of high strangeness really didn't appeal to me, as they seemed to exploit one's natural fears instead of trying to use your intellect to understand the natural world. They kicked in the fight or flight instinct—exactly what I was feeling, a feeling of get out now or be prepared to be fight some mysterious force.

As I put my guitar away and closed up the back of my truck, something new caught my eye, once again, over at Skinwalker Ranch.

The ground was now glowing, and my binoculars revealed eerie bluish flames flickering around the scrub, moving from place to place. I could tell it wasn't a fire, as the flames seemed to kind of undulate and skip around. They reminded me of the Aurora Borealis, which I'd seen many times in Alaska, except these waves of light were smaller and near the ground.

They stopped as suddenly as they started. I stood for awhile, watching, but nothing more seemed to be going on.

It was as if it had never happened.

I got in my truck and drove away, through Fort Duchesne, up to Highway 40, and towards the town of Vernal. I was only a few hours from home. Maybe I should just go back. What would Sarah say if I stumbled into the house in the middle of the night?

I knew she would be happy to see me, so I decided to call her to tell her I was coming home, as much as I hated to wake her.

But her reaction wasn't at all what I expected. I was to find out that things at home weren't at all what I thought.

18. Lost and Alone

· ·

"Hi, hon, is everything OK?" Sarah answered with concern. "It's not like you to call so late."

I could hear yelling and screaming in the background, as well as the sound of music and people talking.

"I'm fine, but what's going on?" I asked, perplexed. Was Sarah having a party? It wasn't at all like her. She was like me, kind of a loner and a hard worker, maybe too serious. She would never party on a week night—or so I thought.

She laughed. "I'm at Mindy and Jordan's. The kids are still up. I kind of threw everyone off balance coming in so late."

Mindy and Jordan were Sarah's niece and her husband. They had two little kids, Dash and Viddie. That was who I could hear making a ruckus in the background, as I now recognized their voices.

"What are you doing over there?" I asked.

"Bad news—we got evicted."

I was stunned. How could we get evicted? We'd bought a little camp trailer, a vintage Shasta, and had fixed it all up. It was small, but cozy, and being able to set it on a friend's rural property out of town a few miles helped us save a ton on rent.

We paid them a small amount each month and kept an eye on their place when they were gone, and it was way cheaper than what we'd been paying in town. Steamboat Springs is a resort town and very expensive.

Sarah added, "The zoning people came out and said we couldn't stay. It's zoned against living in temporary housing, they said. Nobody knew. I had to move it out. It's parked here in Mindy's drive for now, but I'm going to have to find some place to put it."

I groaned, then told Sarah I wanted to come home.

Sarah then asked, "Why, hon? Is everything OK? I'm sleeping on the couch, just so you know. You'd end up on the floor, but I know they'd welcome you here. But the company's sending me to Piceance Basin tomorrow, so I won't be here long."

"Well, I guess I'm not coming home after all," I replied, disappointed. "Since I don't have a home to come to."

I knew Mindy couldn't really put me up, as they had a small two-bedroom house, and I wasn't too eager to sleep on their floor. I also knew we couldn't stay in the trailer while it was parked in their drive.

"I'm going to leave the trailer here until we figure where we can park it. I have a couple of leads. But are you OK?"

I knew Sarah would camp out where she was doing stratigraphy research for an oil company. I suddenly missed her very much.

I then proceeded to tell her about the strange lights. I could feel the tension in my voice, and I knew I'd been more upset than I'd realized.

"They could be earthquake lights," she answered, after listening to my description.

"What's that?" I asked, eager for an answer I could deal with, something not so mysterious and downright scary.

"They're flashes of electricity caused by buildup of stress in rift zones—you know, places where there are deep vertical faults. The current flows to the surface and causes eerie light shows, usually flickering flames or strange orbs of light. It's only been recently that geologists have been able to prove that's what causes them. People have reported them for years as being UFOs or other weird stuff."

"But what causes them, exactly?" I asked. I knew my scientist wife would have an answer. She almost always did, even if she wasn't so sure about Bigfoot—but she tried to keep an open mind. Sometimes I thought I wanted to prove Bigfoot's existence just to convince Sarah.

"OK, it gets pretty deep," she joked. "But seriously, you have these really deep vertical faults that go down into the magma, and the crystal structure of magma produces electricity when under stress. As the magma flows upward through the faults, it's stressed, creating electricity, which flows to the surface, ionizes the air, and creates these weird light displays. It's nothing supernatural at all, just earthquake lights."

"Do you think there's going to be an earthquake there?"

Sarah paused, thinking, and I could hear Mindy telling the kids to get to bed.

"No, I'm not sure what's going on there. I suspect the Skinwalker Ranch is right above a deep rift, but it's not necessarily part of an earthquake zone, per se. It's in a fore-land basin. I'm going to have to ask some of my geology colleagues about this and report back."

She asked where I would go next. I wasn't sure, but Wyoming wasn't very far away—maybe I should go back to Plan B—or was it Plan C?—and go on north to Wyoming, then Montana. Sarah and I said goodbye.

I could see lights in the distance and realized I had almost reached the small town of Vernal, Utah. It was late, and I had no idea where to spend the night. I wanted to spend it with Sarah.

I stopped in the small town and filled my tank, then turned north into the vast darkness of rugged and isolated northeastern Utah, feeling lost and alone, which I pretty much was.

19. Highway of Dreams

· ·

There's something about night driving that can either soothe the soul or make you feel on the edge of nothingness. Being in the cab of a vehicle isolates you from the rest of the world, leaving the mind free to wander beyond its normal confines. It seems like night driving is a form of movement within movement, which makes it almost dreamlike.

I've spent lots of late nights driving in order to meet fishing clients early the next morning in remote areas, and quite often I feel a sense of wonder at the night sky and at how elusive the planet becomes in the dark.

But this night, driving north from Vernal on the blue highway to Flaming Gorge Dam, I felt nothing but loneliness.

My chasing after Bigfoot had gotten me nowhere fast, except to a place where I was questioning my abilities to stay grounded. I'd never felt this way before, and I had no idea why I felt so afflicted, but I guessed it was from just too much strangeness.

When the strangeness wasn't external, like the mountain lion circling my tent, it was internal, like the monk-like figures, and the combination of the two was making me feel lost at sea.

Gone was my self-confidence, my ability to feel like I could cope with most anything. I was barely holding myself together, and the strange lights at Skinwalker were feeling like the final straw—and on top of that, I now knew I had nowhere to call home.

I felt a strong urge to return and help Sarah find a place to put our trailer, but I knew she would be gone by the time I got there, out to Piceance Basin in central Colorado, home of vast reserves of oil and gas, which she was helping locate. Sarah's speciality was sequence stratigraphy, a field in demand by the oil companies. The trailer would be fine, waiting in storage, until I completed my quest.

I've learned through the years that walking is good for me when I feel unsettled, that I can go walk it off, as they say. After a good five or ten mile hike, I come back feeling like my old self again. Maybe my body's too tired at that point to put up with any existential nonsense, but whatever the reason, it works.

But I couldn't just stop and go for a hike, especially since it was dark, so instead I just drove and drove. I would drive it off instead of walking it off.

I drove past Flaming Gorge Dam and its big reservoir, then on up through the small town of Dutch John, and past a sign that read, "Welcome to Wyoming, the Cowboy State."

I'd been through here years ago, and even though it was dark, I knew I was crossing the wide open spaces of high Wyoming desert. I was glad it was late summer, as it was no place to be in the winter—the ground blizzards here were infamous, with nothing in the landscape to stop the blowing snow or to even slow it down.

I now look back and can see I was running away from all the strangeness of the Uintas. It felt dark there, and I wanted light. Even though some of my time there was pleasant, the whole place was beginning to have a strange taint to it. I recognized that it was in my own mind and probably not real, but I had no way to change that. I just wanted to get away.

It's funny how we can develop associations with a place and have feelings that color our perceptions of it, and someone else may feel completely different. I'd been in the Uintas enough to recognize their stunning beauty, and I'd felt a strange sense of peace there, yet it was now gone and I didn't feel comfortable. Was it from the stories I'd heard about Bigfoot and the Skinwalker Ranch?

I didn't think so, as I'd heard lots of stories about Bigfoot even near where I live, up in the Mount Zirkel Wilderness near Steamboat, and I loved hiking there. I had heard almost no stories about the Skinwalker Ranch, I just knew it had some notoriety, and yet it felt weird there. But who knows, maybe it was just me.

After a couple of hours I could once again see lights in the distance, and I knew I was near Rock Springs, Wyoming. Once there, I again stopped for gas, even though I had a half tank. I just didn't want to get on some back lonely highway and run out. I was well aware that a mile in Wyoming is much longer than a mile anywhere else—or so it seemed, anyway.

The town felt lonely and deserted, in spite of its big truck stops and freeway presence, as it set along I-80. I soon left it all behind and continued north on Highway 191. The moon cast a yellowish shadow across the wide expanse of desert, leaving me feeling even more desolate. I suddenly felt like I was in a dream.

I eventually came to a sign indicating there was a rest stop ahead, and I pulled over when I got there. Painted on the pavement in large white letters were the words, "Here Are You."

No one else was around, so I stopped and got out and noted there was nothing there but a few parking spaces and a restroom. I walked over to the large words painted on the pavement and realized I'd been looking at them the wrong way and they were supposed to read, "You Are Here."

I decided I was too tired to continue, so I crawled into the back of my truck, locked the door, and fell into a deep and restless sleep, dreaming that our little camp trailer was floating down an Amazon-sized river with Sarah standing in the door in amazement while I looked on from the shore, helpless to do anything.

I woke as the sun began its slow daily journey across the vast Wyoming landscape, a golden glow barely visible in the east. Soon, the vast open desert emerged from shadow, shimmering in the rising sun.

I stood and savored the openness and light, much like a voyager in a ship's hold might feel upon emerging from days in darkness. The sun! Light!

I knew where I was going now—it was as clear in my mind as the radiant rays that burst through Wyoming's clear skies—I would go visit the Range of Light, Wyoming's Wind River Mountains.

I could barely wait to get there, and I jumped in my truck and took off without even taking the time to make a cup of cowboy coffee.

I was on my way, the previous night's strangeness forgotten.

20. Diggs

I used to really enjoy reading the books of John Muir, the famous naturalist. He was the first to coin the term "Range of Light," referring to California's Sierras.

Muir once wrote, "The mighty Sierra, miles in height and so gloriously colored and so radiant, it seemed not clothed with light, but wholly composed of it, like the wall of some celestial city." Muir was fascinated by light, and his travels and writings reflected that enchantment.

The Sierras are composed primarily of granite, which is famous for its reflective abilities, and thus Muir's description. Interestingly enough, the Wind River Range in Wyoming is made of similar plutonic granite, lifted from immense depths into the skies by similar tectonic forces.

Before Sarah and I were married, we'd spent some time hiking and camping in the Winds, where she had explained the geology to me, much of which I'd forgotten, except for the granite part. And like the Sierras, the Winds had also seen extensive glaciation, which had carved impressive cirques and hanging valleys. I was on my way to those beautiful mountains.

I continued north across Wyoming's wide sweeping high desert and was soon in the tiny town of Eden, then in the similar small town of Farson. Distant jagged peaks ahead and to the east spoke of likewise distant treasures, the bejeweled lakes of the Winds, jumping with cutthroat trout.

Time passed quickly, and I felt like a little kid, eager for adventure. My old self was back.

Before long, I reached the town of Pinedale, official gateway to the Wind River Range. Pinedale has over 1300 lakes in its vicinity, the largest being Fremont Lake, Wyoming's second largest lake. And the Wind River Range claims 15 of Wyoming's 16 highest peaks, and the scenery was stunning.

I stopped in Pinedale to resupply and get gas. And once again, like in Roosevelt, I had an interesting encounter in front of the local grocery store, though this one a bit more personal, as I left with a new friend—one that would tag along on my journey and provide both good and bad company, as well as maybe saving my life, though I didn't know it at the time.

As I walked up to the store, I saw a kid crouched on the curb, holding what appeared to be a small black and white dog. The kid looked to be about 10, and was, like the dog, pretty scruffy. As I approached, he looked up at me.

"Say, mister, would you take my dog?"

I was taken back. I'd never had anyone try to give me their dog before, and the way he said it, it didn't sound like he'd found a stray or anything, but it was just his dog and he wanted to give it away.

I wasn't sure how to respond, but the look of sadness on the young boy's face immediately tugged at my heart. I had a sinking feeling.

I stopped and responded, "Why are you wanting to give your dog away?"

"I don't," he replied with remorse.

"But didn't you just offer me your dog?"

The dog looked to be about six months old, a mix of Border Collie and something I couldn't quite put my finger on, a bit stockier and with a tail that curled up over its back. The pup's face seemed to reflect the misery on the young boy's.

"My dad said if I don't find Diggs a home he's going to take him out and shoot him."

"Oh, man, that's bad. Why would he shoot him?" The sinking feeling I had was sinking deeper.

"Because my dad's like that. He's a..." The boy paused, then continued, "...a shooter."

I changed the subject. "What's his name again? Diggs? Does he dig a lot?"

"Not any more, not since he growed up. He just did that when he was little."

Now the boy was holding the pup close to him, as if not wanting him to go away. The pup squirmed and broke free. I held my hand out and he started licking it.

"See, he likes you."

"Do you think your dad would really shoot him? What does your mom say about that?" I was now sitting on the curb next to them.

"My mom doesn't say nuthin' cause she's gone."

I was afraid to ask what he meant by gone, so I said nothing.

"Well, OK, I'll take Diggs, but under one condition."

I couldn't believe what I was saying.

The boy looked questioning.

I continued. "You have to give me your number and address so I can stay in touch and let you know how Diggs is doing. He'll miss you, you know. Maybe I can even meet up with you sometime so you guys can say hello. What's your name?"

"Tim Watson. My dad owns the gas station. Probably the same one you'll be getting gas from. I hang around there when I'm not in school. The one on the corner over there."

It was indeed the very station I'd just gassed up at.

Tim handed me the dog, which had no leash or collar. The dog immediately went back to Tim's arms.

"OK, look, why don't you bring him over to my truck. Tell you what, let me get some groceries first so he's not sitting alone in there, just in case he tries to dig his way out. You wait here, OK?"

The boy nodded his head, and I went inside. I was soon back out.

"What kind of dog food does he like?" I asked.

"He eats anything," came the reply.

I quickly grabbed some groceries and a bag of dog food, plus some chewies and dog biscuits. I paused, then put a collar and leash in the basket. I couldn't believe this was happening. I'd been wanting a dog, but hadn't really planned on getting one just yet.

Back outside, Tim carried Diggs over to my truck and put him inside the cab. The little dog looked scared as Tim closed the door behind him.

"Has he been in a car before?" I suspected he hadn't.

"No."

"Is he house trained?"

"Yeah. I sneak him into my room at night."

"OK, write your name and address and phone on this piece of paper. I'm heading north, but I live in Colorado and I'm coming back through this way before long. I want to stop and say hello. I'm Rusty, by the way."

Tim wrote down the information and handed me the paper. He shook my hand awkwardly.

"You'll be good to him?" He asked.

"For sure. My wife and I have been talking about getting a dog. We love dogs. I'm a fishing guide and she's a geologist. Between the two of us, he'll be outdoors running around a lot. He'll get lots of love, Tim, don't you worry about that."

For some reason I felt that the dog would probably be getting more love than Tim, sadly enough.

Tim tried to smile, shot a quick glance at Diggs, then started to cry. He turned quickly so I wouldn't see him and ran across the street and on down to the gas station.

Later, talking to Sarah, I could see I'd missed some red flags through all this, but at the time, I was innocent—or maybe naive would be the better word.

I got into the cab, only to see that Diggs had peed all over the truck seat.

21. The Warning

I went back into the store and bought a bunch of paper towels and some spray cleaner, then did my best to clean it all up. Surprisingly enough, it hadn't gone through the seat cover, so I was OK. I could take that off later and wash it. Fortunately, it was the first and only time.

Through it all, Diggs looked incredibly guilty and sorry and sad all at once.

I kept talking to him, telling him it was OK and petting him, and he finally seemed to warm up a bit to me. I drove on over to the city park and put his collar on him kind of tight, as I didn't want to risk him getting away. I then walked him around some, and he seemed to perk up.

"Good boy, Diggsy, good little doggie."

I wondered if he'd been neutered. I suspected not, and sure enough, a quick look confirmed my suspicions. That would be on the list of things to do when I got back. No need to breed more stray dogs in this world, though I had no intentions of letting him run.

He seemed to be incredibly smart, which I knew Border Collies had a reputation for being. He was soon walking around on the leash like an old hand at it, not even pulling.

I took him over to a bush and encouraged him to use it before we got back into the truck.

I then drove over to an outdoors shop I'd noticed, wanting to get some maps and information. I decided to take Diggs in with me, if they'd let me, as I didn't trust him in the truck. If I had to, I could tie him by the door, since I'd only be in there for a few minutes.

I was already feeling the change in my life that would come from having a dog—it hopefully would be mostly for the better, but right then, I wasn't so sure.

One of the clerks said it was OK for Diggs to come in, and the little dog sat obediently while I bought some maps and talked a bit about the Winds and places to camp and hike. The staff was incredibly friendly, at least until the owner showed up.

He took one look at me, one at Diggs, and said, "I hate to tell you this, but I wouldn't recommend taking a dog into the backcountry."

"Why not?" I asked, surprised.

"Dogs are the number one way to get a grizz to come visit your camp. People think they'll scare a bear away, but they have the opposite effect. They'll attract bears to you. We've heard a lot of stories of dogs and grizz, and they don't mix. The dog always gets the short end of the stick—the people, too, sometimes." He looked grim.

"I didn't realize the Wind Rivers had many grizzly bears," I replied.

"They're more in the northern section, but we get a few down at this end. If you go talk to the folks at the recreation shop up north in Dubois, they can tell you some sad tales. They'll give you the same advice. For some reason, grizzly bears are curious about dogs and will often attack them. Probably because the dogs bark at them."

"Should I get a bear bell?" I asked.

"It won't hurt, but you should definitely get some bear spray. But just be safe and don't take him up there at all."

I felt too poor to spend the money on bear spray and bells, no matter how prudent it would be. I left wondering again what to do and where to go. I wanted to go visit the Wind Rivers and do some camping and hiking there, but I sure didn't want to meet up with any grizzlies.

I considered the Winds to be a Bigfoot Hotspot, especially after hearing a few stories from fishing clients, plus I wanted to go explore some. Sarah and I had camped at the famous Cirque of the Towers, but there was so much more to see.

Should I just bag it and go on up to the Tetons? They were stunning mountains and I sure couldn't go wrong with that.

But something tugged at me. I was here to find Bigfoot, and I knew I had a good chance of that in the Winds— probably a better chance than in the Tetons, unless I could get deep into them, and I wasn't really prepared to do any backpacking.

I finally decided I'd go on up into the Wind Rivers and car camp, just do some day hikes, staying close to the popular areas, where grizzlies were probably less likely to go. I knew they tried to avoid humans, so I'd probably be fine by staying on well-hiked trails.

Maybe Bigfoot would find me up in the Winds if I just sat tight and waited for him. Did I really believe that? I didn't think so, but I wasn't so sure.

I thought again of the folklore at the Utah State University archives.

Bigfoot shows himself to those individuals who he feels are ready to see him.

I lifted Diggs back into the truck, as he seemed reluctant to get in, then gave him a chewy, which he sniffed at like he'd never seen such a thing, then went to chewing like crazy. If he'd been able, I think he would've smacked his lips. A few times he would take a break from chewing and look at me with a new light, as if he'd underestimated me.

We were soon on the road to the Big Sandy trailhead and campground, a good 55 miles up a partly paved then gravel road. The Big Sandy was the gateway to the Cirque of the Towers.

It took some driving, plus a lot of willpower to not stop and go fishing in the meandering Big Sandy River that the road paralleled, but we were eventually at the parking lot at the trailhead.

It was packed with cars and people, something I hadn't expected, and I was tempted to turn around. I knew the Cirque was a popular climbing spot, but I was still surprised.

I had noticed a few good camp spots on back down the road a few miles, so I decided to go back there to camp for the night. As usual, the thought of being around a lot of people made me kind of nervous. But since it was only mid-afternoon, I figured Diggs and I could go for a short hike first and check things out.

We'd then go down the road and camp and come back the next day, maybe even climbing up the 10,800-foot Jack-ass Pass to where one can look out onto an awesome view of the Cirque. That alone would be a steep and long hike of seven miles one way, assuming we got that far. If not, we would just go as far as we wanted, then turn back, making it a day hike.

I was excited to take Diggs out on what I assumed would be his first taste of wild country hiking. Little did I know what would happen in just a few short hours, not the next day, and that things would be much wilder than I could have ever expected in my wildest dreams.

22. A Shadowy Visit

Diggs and I headed up the trail, my day pack holding the usual, but this time also some dog biscuits. I would normally take a map and a compass, but I didn't intend to go off-trail.

I knew from when Sarah and I had been here years before that the trail was an easy hike for the first five miles, when you reached Sandy Lake, then got tough after that. But I didn't intend to go to the lake. We wouldn't have time, with it being so late in the day. I mostly just wanted to get out and stretch our legs, my two and Diggs' four.

As we started up the trail, Diggs was so excited that I could barely hold him back. He acted like he'd never been on a hike, and he kept turning and looking back at me like he was wondering what we were doing and if it were for real or not.

Every time someone came by, he wanted to sniff and jump up on them, but I held him back. We didn't see any other dogs on the trail.

After a half-hour of this, he was wearing me out, but he showed no signs of abating. He was one energetic pup, and going on a walk seemed to be the highlight of his short life so far, maybe next to the chewy, anyway. I laughed at his enthusiasm when I wasn't trying to slow him down. For a small dog, he sure had a good pull. Maybe I should hook him to a wagon or something, I thought.

Finally, I'd had enough and stopped near the river to take a break. There was a big rock not far from the bank, and it looked like the perfect place to have a granola bar and dog biscuit.

This late in the summer, the river was shallow and meandered slowly through the meadow. It must've looked enticing to Diggs, as he kept pulling, wanting to go over to the water. He ignored the biscuit I offered him, so I figured he must be thirsty, so I took him to the bank.

Before I could blink, he'd jumped off the edge into the water. I instinctively let go of his leash so as not to follow him in.

He swam a bit, then climbed onto a small island. I maybe could have followed him and caught him without going in over my head, but I wasn't sure, and I didn't want to get wet.

I stood on the bank, calling to him, holding out the biscuit in what I suspected was a useless gesture.

"Diggs, c'mere Diggs, good boy, Diggs."

He stood there, looking at me, and almost came, then turned and looked like he was going to wade through to the other side. He then paused, unsure of the water. I worried that he would get the leash caught on something, and kept encouraging him to come back.

Just then, a hiker came by with a dog. He stopped, seeing Diggs out in the middle of the river. As soon as Diggs saw the other dog, a golden retriever, he jumped into the river and swam back my way, getting out of the water. When he approached the other dog, its owner tried to grab Diggs' leash, but he was too elusive and jumped away, just out of reach.

I ran over, but Diggs wouldn't let me catch him, and even the biscuit wouldn't lure him to me. At one point, I was able to stomp on the end of the leash, but it slipped away from under my foot. Diggs stood just out of reach, looking like this was a game he'd played before and relished—stump the humans.

"Maybe if you start down the trail he'll follow and I can catch him at the parking lot," I told the hiker. He obliged, and continued hiking back to the trailhead, his obedient good dog at his heels and Diggs following, just out of reach. I followed along behind Diggs, hoping to catch him when he wasn't looking, but no such luck.

Before long, we were back at the vehicles, and the hiker's dog jumped into his car. We were hoping Diggs would jump in too, but he was too wary.

Finally, the hiker said he had to leave, apologizing for not being able to stay and help. But there wasn't much else anyone could do. My hope was that eventually the little dog would get tired of his game and let me catch him.

At this point, I went to my truck and got some turkey I'd bought for sandwiches, hoping to use it to lure Diggs. He was interested, but knew it was a trap and came close but managed to avoid me.

I was by now extremely frustrated. I had no idea what to do, except stay in the parking lot until the dog decided to let me catch him, if ever. Even if it meant sleeping there, I would do it, as there was no way I would abandon the dog, frustrated as I was.

It was nearly dark, and still no Diggs. He was laying over in the grass at the edge of the parking lot, but when I tried to approach him, he would casually get up and move to the other edge. By now, it appeared that the day hikers were all back and the cars that remained belonged to climbers or backpackers who wouldn't be back for some time.

It was just me and Diggs, there at the trailhead of the Big Sandy, wasting time that we could've spent playing guitar and chewing dog chewies down at some quiet camp by the river. But no, instead we were playing this game of frustration, me and this little dog I'd just met a few hours before and who was now somehow my responsibility.

I was beginning to think that maybe there was a little more to the Diggs story than I'd been told. I had no idea if Tim's dad was really the type to shoot a dog, but right then and there, I think I could've whacked the little dog with a stick or something, I was so mad.

Of course, there's no way I would do something like that, but my frustration was at a boiling point. Finally, I decided there was nothing more I could do, so I set about making some dinner. I would just have to spend the night there and hope Diggs didn't run off, then try again in the morning. Maybe by then he'd be hungry enough to come to me.

Soon the mosquitoes were out in full force, and between slapping at them and trying to get my propane stove lit, I didn't notice the dark shadow now standing at the edge of the trees watching me.

23. Fleeing Again

I decided to make something that would smell good to a dog, my choice being a package of hot dogs. I would fry them in a pan, letting the smell waft over to Diggs.

I needed to hurry, as I really didn't want to be cooking and cleaning up my stuff in the dark. The hot dogs were soon done, even though somewhat burned, and I ate one, then took another over to Diggs, trying to entice him to come to me.

He was still playing the elusive game, and I had no idea why. What did he think I was going to do to him? Of course, after all this was over and I finally got him home, he took to Sarah like a little shadow and never left her side. But me, that was another story, at least then.

I cleaned up the pan and put everything away, and then put on my headlamp. I was ready to go to bed, but I wanted to give it one more try.

I walked slowly over to where the little dog was curled up in the grasses like he was ready to spend the night there, just like a wild dog or coyote. And speaking of coyotes, I really worried about leaving him out all night, as coyotes can and will kill a domestic dog.

He lay still, and I was beginning to think maybe he was going to let me catch him this time.

"Good boy, Diggs, good boy. Let's stop this stupid game and go to bed, what say? Good little doggie..." I held out a hotdog.

He was motionless, and I was almost within catching distance when he suddenly began to growl. It was a no-nonsense growl, the kind that gives one pause when they hear it coming from a dog, a growl that means I'm going to seriously bite you if you don't back off.

I was shocked. It hadn't even occurred to me that he might bite me, but he sure sounded like he meant it. I felt a sudden wave of fear—what if he went after me? What would I do?

He growled again, and I stepped back, just in time for him to jump up and bolt right by me. I quickly turned just in time to see a huge shadowy figure behind me, not more than thirty feet away, with Diggs lunging at it.

Was it a Bigfoot? It was certainly large enough to be one, and with it standing there on two legs, I wasn't sure. But when it turned and made a swipe at the little dog, I could see it had a big hump on its back.

A grizz! How in hellsbells did I go from having a nice quiet hotdog dinner to being on the line with a grizzly bear? As the adrenaline kicked in, I ran for my truck. I didn't have any kind of weapon, so my only choice for survival was to get away.

The big hump indicated that it had stored a lot of fat for the coming winter, and maybe some of that fat had come from people's camps, as it didn't seem even a little afraid.

But I couldn't leave Diggs! I started the truck and turned on the lights, and now I could get a better look at what was coming down.

The bear was now down on all fours, swatting and trying to get at Diggs, who very deftly always stayed at the bear's rear.

I wasn't sure what to do. If I called Diggs and he actually came to me, I knew the bear could follow.

Grizzly bears are tremendously fast, and I wasn't sure I could even get the little dog into the truck and shut the door before it also got there. And we've all heard the tales of how a bear can rip a car apart if it wants to, so I wasn't even sure we'd be safe while I was getting the truck going.

As I watched in suspense, the little dog circled around the bear, always a few inches from its long yellow claws, almost like it was playing a game. The bear looked really frustrated and angry, and I could relate, having had my own bout with the pup.

I rolled down the window and called Diggs, but, as usual, he ignored me. I could see the bear cock its head towards me, which I wasn't sure I liked, but Diggs was keeping it totally sidetracked. I couldn't bear the thought of seeing the little dog mauled and probably killed by the grizzly.

But before my very eyes, and I really couldn't believe it, I watched him quickly come up behind the bear and bite it on its rear end!

Now the bear made a sound like a combination of a growl and a yip of pain, and tried even harder to grab at the dog. Diggs was fast, I'd grant him that, and he again bit the bear on the rear.

The bear had apparently had enough, as it took off, coming right by my truck, close enough that I at first thought it was coming after me. But it wasn't—it was retreating into the thick forest, Diggs close behind.

I was in shock. The bear was gone, but so was Diggs. Would I ever see the dog again? I waited a few minutes, then carefully opened my door and called for him.

Nothing.

I called over and over, and was about ready to give up. I felt sick. How had this happened? I knew I'd have to spend the night there—no way was I going anywhere without Diggs, even if I had to spend tomorrow looking for him. I wouldn't go back without him, even if it was with his cold lifeless body.

Finally, I saw him coming back. He came right up to the truck, and let me grab his leash. He jumped right into the truck and lay down on the seat next to me. I can't describe the sense of relief I felt.

I now drove down the road, happy to have escaped. Diggs had settled down and was now licking his paws. I grabbed a couple of dog biscuits and gave them to him, and he quickly munched them up. His escapade had made him hungry, so I gave him more.

Had Diggs saved my life? I didn't know. For one thing, I wouldn't have been there in the first place if it hadn't been for him. But I might have been camped nearby, and who knows, maybe that grizz was bold enough to try to break into my truck. I would've been there, sleeping, with no defense.

A bear that's lost its fear of humans and who associates them with food can be very dangerous—but then again, maybe Diggs was responsible for attracting the bear there in the first place.

As I drove on down the road and on back to Pinedale, it occurred to me that once again I was on the run, though this time I had good reason to be. This whole adventure seemed like a repeat of me going to a place then running away from it. I knew that wasn't entirely true, but it was beginning to feel that way.

Whether I had a legit reason to run or not was irrelevant. I felt no closer to determining if Bigfoot was real than when I'd started, but I had proved for sure that there were grizzly bears in the southern Wind Rivers.

Things were different this time, though, I thought. This time, I had Diggs, a partner in crime. Maybe he would settle me down, make me less afraid. I'd been wishing I had a dog, and I'd wanted to consult with Sarah first, but sometimes things don't happen exactly the way you want them to. I now knew the little dog had way more courage than I did.

Once I arrived in Pinedale, I pulled into a motel parking lot, grabbed Diggs, and climbed into the back of my pickup. I was happy to be in civilization, and even if someone came out and told me I couldn't sleep there, I was better off than where I'd been.

No one bothered me, and I slept like a baby, Diggs curled up next to me, the parking lot lights revealing his forearm laying across his chewy as if guarding it from a grizzly bear.

24. The Truth Will Out

I woke to a spectacular dawn, the sky lit up in a million shades of pink and red. I knew a storm was probably moving in.

Red sky at night, sailor's delight. Red sky at morning, sailor take warning.

I once read that this little rhyme was over 2,000 years old and helped forecast the immediate weather pretty much as accurately as any weatherman. It's based on the fact that the reddish glow of sunrise or sunset is caused by particles and clouds, and forecasting can be done by knowing which direction the winds move.

Since storms move from west to east in the mid-latitudes, seeing the glow in the evening means the storm's already moved through, whereas morning glow means the storm's on its way in, coming from the west. In other words, a reddish sunset shows that the storm is on the west side, or the same side as the sunset, moving away from you, whereas a morning glow foreshadows an approaching storm.

It was time to keep going north. I wasn't far from the Tetons, and though they seemed pretty inaccessible, I wanted to go see them again. Besides, they were on the way to Montana.

I had lots of good associations with Montana, since I often guided fishing trips there, and right then, it felt about as close to home as I could get, seeing my real home was gone. And I had that rendezvous up in the Bridgers, not that I wanted it.

I took Diggs for a little walk, careful to not let him get away, then went to the McDonald's drive-through and got us both a breakfast burrito. He at first acted like I was trying to poison him, but finally tasted it, then swallowed it almost whole and looked at me appreciatively.

Where had this young dog learned to herd a bear like that, and not just any bear, but a grizz? It just didn't seem like a dog would know that. It must be the Border Collie in him, I decided. I knew they were smart dogs and bred for herding, but herding grizzly bears?

As we left Pinedale, something clicked. I recalled a story one of my fishing clients had told me about a dog he had that had actually chased a Bigfoot away from camp up in British Columbia. I had at first found his story totally incredible, but when he educated me about Russian Bear Dogs, I could believe it.

I'd never even heard of the breed before that, and now I suspected I had one. Also known as Karelian Bear Dogs, the breed came from Finland, where they were bred exclusively to hunt and chase bears.

They were fearless dogs, and some of the national parks were now starting to use them to educate bears about staying away from humans. The rangers and dogs would hike together, and when they saw a bear, the dogs would teach the bears that humans meant trouble by biting them and running them off. I knew Glacier National Park and also Yellowstone were using the dogs, sometimes also on moose.

It made sense. That's why I couldn't quite place what breed Diggs was—and bear dogs do have a resemblance to Border Collies, though bear dogs have tails that curl up over their backs, just like Diggs. But they also have similar black and white markings to a Border Collie.

I turned around and headed back to Pinedale, then pulled into Tim's dad's gas station. I parked next to the building and got out. I wasn't too eager to meet someone who had threatened to shoot a dog, but I needed more information.

As I went into the building, I saw Tim sitting behind an old beat-up desk. He appeared to be fiddling with some kind of hand-held video game, and when he saw me, his face turned white as a sheet. I thought for second he might bolt.

"Hi, Tim," I said.

"You bringing Diggs back already?" He looked worried.

"No, no, he's fine. He's a good dog. I'm just back because I need to know where you got him."

Tim looked at his feet and started fidgeting. He paused, then said, "Some guy getting gas gave him to me."

"How long ago was that?"

"I dunno. Last week."

"So, you only had him for a week? Where was the guy from?"

"I dunno."

"Do you think he might've been stolen?"

Now Tim looked even whiter, if possible. He answered quickly. "No way. I dunno."

"I think he might've been stolen because he's a pretty rare breed of dog."

"What is he?" Tim asked. "I didn't steal him, honest. This guy was coming through town and he told me he was too much of a handful for him and that Diggs needed a kid and did I want him? I said, sure, but my dad decided he didn't like Diggs chasing everybody that came through the station. I tied him up, but he kept getting away, and he wouldn't let me catch him. I knew if I told you all that you wouldn't take him, that's all."

"I believe you, Tim. It's OK. I just want to know Diggs' history, that's all. Any idea where the guy was going or coming from?"

"I dunno. He drove that way." Tim pointed south.

Just then, a tall man with dark hair came into the office from the garage area, wiping his hands on an oil rag. I could tell he was Tim's dad, as they looked like carbon copies of each other.

"Morning, sir," he nodded to me. "Anything I can help you with?"

"This here's the guy who took Diggs," Tim said.

"Oh, that was sure nice of you. I'm Gary, Gary Watson. I guess you've met my son, Tim."

Gary and I shook hands, then he continued.

"We had a bit of a problem with Diggs. We all liked him just fine, but he's just a bit too hyper for life here with us. He chases everything that moves. And Tim needs to learn to ask permission before he takes on a responsibility like that." He gave Tim a stern look.

For some reason, Gary Watson didn't strike me as someone who would shoot dogs, but I guessed you never knew.

"Well, I found out last night that he will indeed chase anything," I replied, then told them about the grizz encounter and my theory that Diggs was a Karelian Bear Dog, and since they were very rare and valuable, my suspicions that he'd been stolen.

Gary looked surprised, and Tim looked somewhat vindicated.

"See, Dad, I told you he was special."

Tim's dad was silent for a moment, then said, "Well, every time your mom goes to Jackson, you get something or other going. Next time, you're going up there with her."

"My mom's a teacher and she sometimes goes away for seminars or whatever," Tim explained. "I take advantage, I know, Dad, but you're just such a softie..."

Tim was grinning at his dad, who looked a bit flustered. I took a chance and asked, "You were going to shoot the dog?"

I had to know what kind of person I was dealing with, though I wasn't sure why. I just wanted to know.

Now Gary gave Tim a look. "You told him that?"

"I was just trying to get him a home, like you told me," Tim replied, looking chagrined at being caught in his lie.

"Well, we're going to have a talk about that one when your mom gets home."

I could tell Tim was in trouble, but for some reason, I didn't think it would amount to much. It appeared Tim's mom was the heavy in the family, if there even was one.

"Well, tell you what," I said. "Let me give you my number, and if anything further comes up about the dog, give me a call, OK?"

I handed Gary one of my fly-fishing business cards.

He looked at it, then whistled.

"You're a fly-fishing guide? Man, I've been wanting to go do that for years. My grandfather was a game warden here, and I used to go with him to stock lakes when I was a kid. Never forgot that. I'm going to be giving you a call. Where do you guide?"

"All over," I answered. "Give me a call when you want to go out, and I can let you know where we have plans. I go all over—Colorado, Montana, Utah, but I've never fished around here much. Maybe we can work out a trade—I can teach you the art of fly-fishing and you can turn me onto some good fishing holes."

"And I'll go, too," Tim stated matter of factly. "I'll get to see Diggs that way."

He then disappeared and I knew he was over at my pickup window, saying hello to the dog.

"I need to figure out where Diggs came from," I said to Gary. "I have a feeling someone's missing that little dog."

Gary nodded his head and agreed to call if he got any news. With that, I said my goodbyes, and Diggs and I got back on the road, again heading north.

I was beginning to wonder if I'd ever make it to Montana, yet alone see anything like a Bigfoot.

25. Bear Dogs

As I drove along, Diggs now fast asleep, I began to question my wisdom in taking the little dog. Would he completely foil my attempts at Bigfooting by making them wary and unwilling to show themselves? Or would he attract them to me, then chase them off?

I also began to worry about the possibility of him getting injured or worse, especially the way he'd refused to come. If he were in some kind of danger, and not necessarily from a Bigfoot, as that was pretty unlikely, but he wouldn't come to me, what might happen? I also worried about losing him.

I decided I needed to work with him, to try and train him. He was smart and there was no reason why he shouldn't learn quickly, even though I suspected I would have to outsmart him and untrain his bad habits. I wasn't sure I was smarter than he was, to be honest.

And what about the possibility that he'd been lost or stolen?

I knew Sarah was out in the field by now and wouldn't have a cell signal, so I called my friend Zoey in Logan.

Maybe she could help me out. I needed to know more about these bear dogs, and I also needed help finding if the dog was lost or stolen. That would mean having an internet connection and the time to do some research.

I called Zoey and explained the situation. She immediately tried to talk me into coming back to Logan to sort things out, but I told her I was too far afield—too far distance wise and too far off track of my original mission. She understood and said she'd call me back.

Back on the road again. It seemed like I was spending more time getting on and off the road than I was searching for Bigfoot.

I have to admit that I was somewhat jealous—I'd spent a lot of time sitting around campfires listening to my fly-fishing clients tell about their own encounters with Bigfoot, but to date I'd never had one, unless you could call a few sketchy experiences I'd had Bigfoot encounters.

I thought back to the shadowy figure in the woods near the cabin back in the Uintas—Bigfoot? I don't know, maybe, but seeing how a guy came from that direction later on an ATV, it was unlikely. And the figures wearing monks' robes? Just a wild dream, though it seemed real.

I wanted to know if Bigfoot were real or not, and it didn't seem I was getting much closer to finding out.

I reached over and patted Diggs' head, and he wagged his tail, then scooted over next to me and put his head on my leg, promptly falling back to sleep. For being such a pain, I was sure getting attached to him fast.

We drove along, soon passing the turnoff to the tiny village of Cora—it was actually more like a pit stop with a few buildings than a real town. I hesitated. I knew the road went to the headwaters of the Green River, the very same river I'd camped near only a few weeks ago way south of here in the desert and had the mountain lion walk around my tent.

The road eventually ended at Upper Green River Lake and the unforgettable Square Top Mountain, a huge chunk of granite that reflected in the lake like a moody painting by Albert Bierstadt, the famous 19th century landscape painter.

In fact, I'd grown up with a painting of that very scene that hung in my grandpa's living room, and I knew it by heart. It showed Square Top reflecting in the lake with a big grizzly bear looking at it from the shore. I'd seen numerous photos of the lake, and I knew Bierstadt had made a journey into the region in 1859, but I had never been able to find any information about that particular painting.

I often wondered if my grandfather hadn't owned an original and didn't know it. If so, it would have been worth a fortune, and I often wondered what became of it, but it was probably just a print.

I was reminded of the time I'd climbed the mountain in Colorado named after the famous painter, Mount Bierstadt, barely a Fourteener at 14,065 feet and famous for the impossible willow marsh you have to navigate at the trailhead.

I'd met a guy on top who told me how he'd seen a Bigfoot in the marsh the previous evening. I had always intended to try to find out more about Bigfoot sightings in that area, but never had.

Anyway, I'd always wanted to go see Square Top Mountain, and I almost turned, but something kept me going, and that something was knowing I was running out of time—I would save the quest for Square Top for another trip. This trip was dedicated to Bigfoot—well, from now on it was, anyway. No more sidetracks. And my month of time off was rapidly coming to a close.

The drainage that feeds the headwaters of the Green is also the dividing point between the Winds and the Gros Vent Mountains, another wilderness I'd sworn I would explore some day. Too many mountains, too little time, but I could now see the Gros Vents to my right, and, like the Winds, they were beautiful and very enticing.

Interestingly enough, when one thinks of mountains, they tend to think of places like Colorado or the Sierras, not Wyoming, but Wyoming's mountains are truly world class, and I was quickly forgetting being homesick.

I had just come to the little town of Bondurant when my phone rang. I could tell from the caller ID it was Zoey. I answered, wondering what she'd come up with about Diggs.

"OK, Rusty, here's the scoop on the Bob Daddy-O," Zoey said.

"What's a Bob Daddy-O?" I asked, puzzled.

"Oh, don't get all hung up on that, it's just something silly Tom always says. Anyway, there's a place in the Bitterroot Valley in Montana where they raise and train Karelian Bear Dogs. I talked to them, and I think you may have a problem on your hands."

She paused to let that sink in, then continued.

"These dogs were bred to hunt. They told me it's very difficult to get them to bond with you, as they were bred to leave their owner and find game. They're very independent. They said they have people call them frequently trying to find homes for their bear dogs, as they don't have the time it takes to train them. Seems most people think they got a regular type dog, but they didn't."

I felt a little defensive. I could train Diggs. There was no way I was going to get rid of him.

"What about chasing bears?" I asked.

"Well, they said that not all bear dogs are good at that, just a few. Maybe one or two in a litter at the most."

I felt a sense of pride. "Diggs knew exactly what to do."

Zoey seemed to not have heard me and replied, "Listen to this part. First, the gal I talked to said you could come up there and visit and she would show you some things about training, but she also said to tell you it can take thousands of hours—did you hear that?—thousands of hours just to train them to come to you. They're bred to leave you, not to come. They're hunters. Rust, I think you need to go on up there and visit, and keep an open mind about finding Diggs a good home."

I felt irritated. "He *has* a good home."

"OK, but they jump fences, dig out, bark a lot, and are not always good pets, especially if left alone. And they shed a lot. And sometimes they can be really aggressive to other dogs. They need tons of exercise. Rusty..."

"OK, OK," I replied testily. "I'll go visit them. Tell me how to get there. Is there anything good about these dogs?" I was being facetious, but Zoey didn't pick up on it.

"Sure, they're really smart and have lots of energy. Actually, that's probably also their main problem—they're smart and have lots of energy. But they are beautiful dogs. But OK, she's in Spencer, Montana..."

"OK, but did you happen to find out anything about Russian or Finnish Bear Dogs?"

"I did. I had the same question. She said they're all the same breed. The dogs were originally bred in a part of Finland called Karelia, and that's all now part of Russia."

"Oh, I wondered. OK, thanks for the info. Did she know of any missing bear dogs?"

"No, but she's going to check around. There aren't that many of them, and the owners tend to network. I hope you'll stop back here on your way down. But wait, what did you say about chasing a bear? Your dog chased a bear?"

I had lost the signal. I was entering Hoback Canyon, and would soon be in Jackson.

For some reason, I'd found Zoey really irritating, and instead of being grateful for the information, I was wishing I hadn't talked to her. Maybe it was better being in denial, as I really wanted things to work out with Diggs. On the other hand, the more information I had, the more likely it was that I could make it all work, so I guess it was all good. But I was glad we were cut off.

As evening fell, I could see a band of gray across the sky behind me, and I realized the sky had quickly clouded over. The summer grasses along the road were beginning to sway in the breeze, and it looked like there was definitely a storm coming in.

I knew there was a Forest Service campground somewhere ahead along the river, if I remembered correctly, and it would be a good place to spend the night. Jackson wasn't that far ahead, and there was no way I could afford anything there, probably not even a cup of coffee, as it was too pricey.

I nearly drove by the campground before I could stop, but managed to pull in at the last minute. There were a few people there, but I soon found a spot, gave Diggs dinner and opened a can of Polish sausages for myself, took him for a short walk, then crawled into the back of the truck with him at my side.

The wind howled through the night, rocking me and Diggs and the truck, but I didn't care. I felt a new resolve— having Diggs had triggered something new in me, a new determination. Now that I had a friend and guardian, I was determined to find Bigfoot, and I knew one of the most likely places was nearby—some of the most remote and untouched country in North America.

Tomorrow, I would gear up to go backpacking, just me and Diggs. We would get as close to the southeast corner of Yellowstone National Park as possible, the same country where Yellowstone Ranger Action Jackson had supposedly seen Bigfoot, an area also rich in grizz.

And if we accidentally crossed into the park and a ranger asked about my lack of a permit, I could say Diggs ate it—you know how these bear dogs are.

I felt a sense of elation—I was finally ready for whatever adventure might come my way.

26. Slide Lake

. . . .

The next day I woke to a dreary drizzle. The wind had died down, only to be replaced with a steady cold rain reminding me that autumn was just around the corner.

I was soon in Jackson, where my previous night's elation was displaced by depression. I knew Jackson was a tourist trap and that dealing with the traffic and people would be culture shock for me, but I'd made it through my stay in Logan, which has some of the worst traffic I'd ever seen, so I wasn't too worried.

What I didn't expect was the sticker shock that came with trying to gear up for a backpacking trip in one of the West's most expensive towns.

It had been years since I'd packed in anywhere, except for day trips, and my old backpacking equipment was long gone, a victim to a yard sale when we'd moved into the little trailer and had to lighten our load. What I'd had was totally outdated, a Lowe's external frame pack that I'd bought in a yard sale years ago, so I hadn't minded parting with it.

But after looking in several outdoors stores in Jackson, and even going to a second-hand store, I knew my backpacking plan was doomed from the git-go. I simply couldn't afford to gear up, not unless I wanted to sell my truck and hitchhike home.

After a couple of hours of shopping, to no avail, I felt sorry for Diggs having to sit in the truck and decided to just go camp for a few days and hope the weather would break. It was raining too hard to go into the backcountry anyway, unless I also wanted to gear up with waterproof gear, which I also couldn't afford.

I was reminded of the beginning of my expedition in Colorado, where Mark and I had basically set in the rain most of the time in Sunlight Camp. I wasn't looking forward to more of the same, as it would get really boring with just my own company and nothing to do.

I stopped at a general type country store on the edge of Jackson and bought a long ten-foot lead for Diggs, something you might use on a horse instead of a dog. I also bought a big bag of buffalo jerky. I would spend some of my time weatherbound working with the little dog, trying to teach him to come to the Zen of treats.

Finally, after wandering around in a bookstore for a bit, I headed up towards Slide Lake, back on the other side of the valley, in the Gros Vent Mountains. Usually, the road to the little town of Kelly provided lots of great views of the Tetons, but that day, everything was cloaked in gray clouds.

The Gros Vent Road follows the Gros Vent River, and typically one can see herds of bison along the way, but they seemed to be feeling like I did, wanting to hide out, and we saw nary a one. I did see a lone coyote crossing the wide valley floor, and Diggs' ears perked up when he noticed it, but he didn't seem all that interested. I think he felt like I did, a little depressed with the weather.

I'd camped by Slide Lake years before and hoped there would be an opening at the Atherton Creek Campground, which set on the lake's shore. This time of year, it was likely to be full.

After reaching the little town of Kelly, the road began winding through a small canyon and eventually reached a large lake—Slide Lake. Sure enough, I got lucky and there was an open camp spot, probably due to the weather.

I hated to have to pay to camp, especially given my daily deteriorating financial status, but I also had no desire to go looking for a camp spot in this weather with the roads turning to muck. At least the road up to the camp was paved.

I decided not to set up my tent, but instead put a tarp over the picnic table and set my solar lantern out in an act of defiance. Maybe it would make the sun come out, though I doubted it.

I noted several signs about storing your food in the bear-proof containers and wondered how often bears visited camp. Probably black bears, I mused to myself, though I knew this was also grizzly country.

For some reason, the thought of grizz didn't seem as disconcerting here in a campground as it did up in the Winds, maybe because there were more people around to deter bears. But that hadn't saved the poor guy who'd been killed in his tent not too long before up in a similar campground in Yellowstone.

I had scored a nice site in a small grove of aspen right down near the beach, but the rain made all of that pretty much irrelevant. Maybe, if the weather changed, I could take Diggs for a swim.

Slide Lake was formed in 1925 when a huge landslide took down most of the side of Sheep Mountain above the valley where the lake now sets, forming a huge 200-foot high dam on the Gros Vent River. You can still see the huge scar on the mountain above the lake—well, when it's not raining, anyway.

Two years later, part of the dam failed, sending a wall of water down the valley and wiping out the town of Kelly, which has since been rebuilt. The lake is much smaller now.

I sat on the edge of the picnic table under the tarp, restless and depressed. My grand adventure searching for Bigfoot in Yellowstone was thwarted, at least for now, and I was again feeling like the whole thing was a failure.

The line from the folklore story at the university again came to mind:

Bigfoot shows himself to those individuals who he feels are ready to see him.

It just didn't make sense. How could Bigfoot possibly know when someone was ready to see him?

I recalled the story of a fellow named Ron Mower, a construction worker who lives in the small town of Orangeville, Utah, over on the edge of the Wasatch Plateau. In an interview in 1997 with Salt Lake City's *Deseret News*, Ron told the reporter he'd seen Bigfoot nine different times during the years from 1968 to 1990, either in the Uintas or near his home.

"They choose the time for when you can see them," he said. "I've never really hunted for one."

I'd read that report, which interviews another Bigfoot enthusiast, a man named Jack Lapseritis, who claimed a number of paranormal things about Bigfoot, basically saying, "They were brought here millions of years ago by their friends, the star people." Some friends, I thought wryly.

As I sat there in the rain, I had Diggs on the long lead, and I would gently call to him to come, then give a little tug. When he responded, I would give him a small piece of jerky as a treat. He seemed to be catching on quickly, though I doubted he would actually listen to me if he were free to run—he'd be too busy hunting, was my guess.

Anyway, there was something about what people like Mower and Lapseritis believed about Bigfoot that bothered me.

I really did believe that Bigfoot was, like all other creatures on Earth, a product of many years of evolution, perhaps descended from Gigantopithecus, the supposedly extinct genus of ape that existed as recently as 100,000 years ago in southeast Asia. The fossil record suggests that Giganto stood around nine feet tall and weighed in at around 1200 pounds, which could definitely have been Bigfoot ancestral stock.

To hear others talk about Bigfoot as something that belonged on Skinwalker Ranch was—to me, anyway—moving its existence from the realm of scientific possibility into that of superstition and imagination. Did I believe aliens existed? I wasn't sure, but to connect them with Bigfoot seemed dubious, at best.

In that interview, Lapseritis also said that the reason conventional Bigfoot investigators (like me) hadn't found Bigfoot yet was because their belief was limited to viewing the creature as "simply a relict hominid that never became extinct."

I was somewhat irritated at this belief, which I'd heard more than once from others.

The rain had let up some, so I took Diggs down to the lake shore. Should I let him go? It would be fun to throw a stick and watch him swim out and get it—he needed some exercise, and a walk didn't look to be forthcoming in the rain.

I walked down to the beach, scoping it out, and since there wasn't anyone else there eager to get soaking wet in the rain, I decided to let Diggs go play in the water. I released him just in time to see two very large and very dark eyes set in the middle of a very large and very dark furry head looking out from the willows next to the lake.

I tried to grab Diggs, but it was too late. He'd seen it, too, and was gone.

27. Deja Vu All Over Again

· ·

I couldn't believe it—talk about bad timing! I, in my infinite stupidity, had released a Russian Bear Dog the very instant a buffalo (technically a bison) had decided to come to the lake for a drink.

If what Zoey had told me was true, and I had no reason to believe it wasn't, Diggs would take to chasing that buffalo as he had to eating buffalo jerky, and who knows when (and if) I would ever see him again?

Buffalo were not creatures to be trifled with, and even though Diggs had staved off a grizzly, who knows what an angry buffalo might do to him?

I called, but of course he was gone. I could hear a mighty crashing through the bushes and was glad that he'd apparently taken the animal by surprise and it was running, not charging, though I knew it could turn on Diggs in a mere second.

OK, he'd chased off a grizzly and now a buffalo—what was next, a moose? Moose were the very worst on my list, or at least second to a grizzly, for being dangerous. One of my greatest fears as a fisherman was to startle a moose feeding in the shallows of a lake, hidden in the willows, and I was always very careful when fishing in areas where there could be one. They had stomped more than one person and dog to death.

I called again, but it was a waste of time. Should I get in my truck and go looking for him? From the sound of it, he'd chased the buffalo across the main road and on up the hill through the thick brush.

I knew there were huckleberries up there, as I'd picked some last time I was here, so maybe Diggs would run into a black bear while he was at it. There was nothing like a dog chasing wildlife to ruin the serenity of the forest—and the serenity of the wildlife, too, I guess.

Maybe Zoey was right and the little dog was too much for me. I had a sinking feeling that whoever had given Diggs to Tim back in Pinedale had come to the same conclusion.

After kicking a log and cussing a few times, I walked back to my camp. There was nothing I could do. I knew I couldn't talk Diggs into coming back until he was ready, and I had no idea where he even was at this point. And to make things worse, it had again started pouring.

It was now getting late, and the overcast skies made it feel even later. I decided to make dinner and just hope the dog would come back. If he didn't, well, at least we were in an area where there were people on an ongoing basis and maybe someone would eventually find him, though I didn't intend to leave without him.

I was now even more depressed, as well as being disgusted and embarrassed. I hated it when dogs chased wildlife, and I never intended to have a dog like that. Why had

I let him go? How many times did it take for me to learn he was untrustworthy and marched to a different drummer?

When and if he came back, maybe it would be time to take him on up to the woman in Spencer who knew about bear dogs. She could probably find him a home where they knew how to train them.

I sat down dejectedly at the picnic table and ate a peanut butter and jelly sandwich, wishing I had a bowl of hot chili instead. The rain was now really coming down, and I kept having to bail the tarp, as it would bulge in the middle from the water, pulling on the rope I'd used to tie it to the nearby trees.

As I was bailing it, trying not to get too wet, I noticed that someone was walking down the path to my camp. I figured it was the campground host coming to tell me I would have to leave because my dog was chasing wildlife. As they came closer, I could see it was an older woman wearing a rain poncho.

She silently lifted her hand in a greeting, kind of like an alien in a movie, then congenially said hello.

"Good evening. I'm Amy. My husband and I are the camp hosts here." She now held her hand above her eyes to shield them from the rain. "We've been getting visits from a black bear and I'm just walking around making sure everyone knows to keep their food in the bear canisters."

I nodded in agreement, glad she hadn't seen Diggs chasing the wildlife. I then begrudgingly decided I needed to alert her, in case she saw him.

"I have a young bear dog that I just got, and he chased a buffalo away from camp here just awhile ago. I stupidly let him off-leash to get some exercise. If you see him, will you come get me?"

"A buffalo?" She seemed exasperated. "We haven't had buffalo come into camp before. Oh boy, not something new to deal with." She paused, then it seemed to register what I'd said about having a bear dog.

"You have a bear dog? Oh, I'd love to meet him. I know one of the rangers up in Yellowstone who's now using them out on the trail."

"I just got him. He's only about six months old and hasn't learned a lot yet."

"Well, I hope he comes back. I'll watch for him. But keep an eye out. This bear is full-grown and pretty big. If it keeps coming around, we're going to have to get it trapped and relocated."

We talked a bit longer, then she turned and walked back up the path. It was now pretty dark, but I walked back down to the lake shore, calling Diggs while watching for bears.

Nothing. I felt sick. I hoped he wasn't lost, but he didn't know the country at all, and I had no idea how he could find his way back in the dark. Just enough light from the now-full moon broke through the clouds for a moment, revealing a thick layer of fog over the lake. It all looked eerie and desolate.

Finally, after calling for Diggs over and over, I gave up and crawled into the back of my truck and pulled on my longjohns. My clothes were soaked, so I draped them over the wheelwells inside, hoping they would dry.

I left the back of the topper open in the hopes that Diggs would come back and jump in with me. The rain seemed to have abated a little, and it gradually tapered off until all was silent.

I lay there awake for some time, thinking of Diggs and worrying about him, then started slowly drifting off to sleep.

Sometime in the night, something woke me, and I sat up on my elbows, trying to see into the shadows out the back of the truck. Was it the bear?

I listened. Now, far in the distance, I could hear what sounded like woodknocking—whack, whack—two times, then a return—whack, whack. It was so faint I wasn't sure what I was hearing, but I swore it was woodknocking.

And it was what I heard next that kept me from sleeping the rest of the night—the faint sound of a dog barking, and it sounded like it was coming from the same direction as the woodknocking.

It felt hopeless. There was nothing I could do but hope Diggs was OK.

28. The Night Hike

As the clouds moved back in, the night became darker and more ominous. I strained to hear, but all was silent—the barking and woodknocking had stopped. And as I lay there, I thought I could now hear something in the bushes next to my truck.

I was half-afraid to turn on my headlamp, but I had to see if it was Diggs. I hoped it wasn't the bear the camp host had mentioned.

I flashed my light around, but it was nothing, maybe just a breeze that had kicked up some leaves or something. It then dawned on me that everything was wet, so it would be hard for the breeze to kick up anything. Yet I hadn't seen a thing.

I lay there, tense, and suddenly had a flashback to a similar time—similar because it was dark and I was scared. I lay there, thinking and remembering.

Before I met Sarah, I used to go night hiking. It was kind of a crazy thing to do, in retrospect, but I wanted to be in shape for climbing, which I enjoyed, and it seemed like the days were always filled and I didn't get the exercise I wanted.

I loved the solitude at night after the world had slowed down, even on trails that were busy during the day, and the night sky was something to behold. If I was lucky, I'd typically see a meteor or two blazing in blue or green across the sky.

I usually went up a small valley not far from where I was living near Carbondale, Colorado—a place called Marion Gulch. It had once been the site of a small coal mining town, but since then, most of the buildings had either been moved or were crumbling into the ground. It was a beautiful hike, along a small creek and through stands of aspen.

One day, I had some extra time at lunch and went hiking instead of waiting to go after dark. I veered off-trail into a small meadow, where I saw something like I'd never seen before—the meadow was circled by large aspens, and every one had long claw marks in its bark, some stretched way above my head. The trees had either grown or the bears that had left the claw marks were very tall. I suspected the former.

As I looked up into the aspen branches, I saw a bear stand. It was old and falling apart, but it confirmed that I'd stumbled into a place bears liked to frequent, or maybe had before the hunters came, anyway.

I kind of tip-toed out of the meadow, my sense of awareness much higher than it had been. I really hadn't thought much about bears before that, as Colorado has only black bears, and they typically are shy.

It's always a change of perspective for me to leave my Colorado home and hike in places like Wyoming or Montana, as I have to garner my courage to go into grizzly-bear country. It's not that the grizz might kill you that scares me, it's more *how* they might kill you. Unlike a black bear, who will kill primarily from fear or self-protection, the grizz typically kills for food.

I'm not afraid of black bears, though the statistics will tell you they kill more people each year than the grizzly, but that's primarily because the blacks are more common and are found in more places across the country. But most blacks are afraid of people. Grizzlies will often stay away from humans, but more out of prudence than fear.

Anyway, I went on for a short hike up Marion Gulch, then went back to work. The next evening, I decided to go for a nice long night hike, but instead of going up through Marion Gulch, I decided to follow a road I'd seen while in the bearclaw meadow the day before.

By the time I was at the place where I parked my car, it was nearly dark, and I cut down through a small wetlands instead of going up the trail, as I normally did. This was new territory to me, and as it was still evening, I noticed something white nearby.

I stopped to examine it, only to see it was a small rounded white wooden marker. I'd found an old grave! As I shined my light around, I saw several other old markers, some so worn that there was no name, all growing entwined by weeds and vines. I'd stumbled on the overgrown abandoned graveyard for the long-abandoned town of Marion!

I soon crossed a small wetland, then met up with the road I'd seen from the bearclaw meadow the previous day. The road looked fairly recent, like it had maybe been cut for logging trucks, as it was wide and smooth. Now that I was on it, I turned off my light and started up it, able to make out the edges of the road in the dark.

It was soon pitch black, but I was still able to barely make out the road, which by now was in deep timber, tall pines blocking out all but the stars straight overhead. I normally liked to hike in more open country, and I began to feel an unsettled sense. I wrote it off to the darkness all around and continued on.

I'd gone about a quarter-mile further when suddenly, from nowhere, a strange foreboding hit me like I'd walked into a brick wall, it was that sudden. I stopped and listened, but heard nothing.

Having grown up pretty much in the wilds, I've learned to trust my senses, my intuition, and they were now telling me to flee, to get out as soon as possible. I knew not to run, for if there were a predator nearby, running would kick in its chase instinct. I needed to remain very quiet, just like when that mountain lion had circled my camp in the desert—at least before I'd broken out the rock and roll concert.

I've been in some pretty hairy circumstances, places where my life literally hung by a thread, and yet I've never been as afraid as I was that night, and I didn't even know what I was afraid of!

I slowly turned and began walking quickly down the trail. Every so often I would turn to see what was behind me, but I didn't see anything, as it was too dark. I didn't want to show whatever it was my location, so I kept my light off and followed the faint outline of the road until I was back at the wetlands.

I needed my light to navigate the shallow water, so I turned it on and crossed as fast as I could, then walked past the graveyard and literally ran the last 100 feet to my car, jumping in and locking the door, no longer able to control my panic.

And even though I was now inside my car, I was still panicked. I turned around and took off, still expecting to see something, but there was nothing there. I was all the way back home before I stopped shaking. And all this was long before I had any real thoughts of Bigfoot.

What had it been? I had no idea, but I had to trust my instincts and believe it was something real. I believe that many thousands of years living as hunter-gatherers in the natural world hardwired humans to pick up cues on a sub-conscious level, though many of us no longer pay them any mind.

Had it been merely a deer, like had scared me on the trek back from Logan Peak on my more recent night hike? I didn't know, but I didn't think so.

And so, that night, there in the back of my truck, wondering where Diggs was and what was making the bushes move, I felt that same sense of fear, though maybe not as strong.

This time, there was no fleeing—I couldn't just run away and abandon the little dog.

So, I lay there, heart pounding, unable to sleep, waiting for the morning light.

29. The Clearing

· ·

Morning came and I woke, not sure where I was—Marion Gulch? Then I remembered—Slide Lake. I had managed to get a little sleep. I got up, hoping to see Diggs, but no such luck.

The weather had cleared, and even though there was still a lot of fog over the lake, I could see blue sky to the west. I quickly dressed, grabbed a granola bar and Diggs' leash, then headed down to the beach.

I walked a long ways one way, then a long ways the other. Slide Lake was a big lake, and I once thought I saw a moose ahead of me in the distance, but it faded into the fog. I was looking for tracks—Diggs' and whoever else's I might find, but all I saw were what looked like duck or some kind of bird tracks.

I finally gave up and returned to camp. I got into my truck and drove around the campground and even down to the boat ramp. There were hardly any other campers around. I guessed that the soggy weather had run everyone out.

Finally, I turned and drove out on the main road and the six or so miles back towards Kelly, the whole time looking everywhere for Diggs. Nothing.

I drove slowly back to the campground, down to my camp, then out the other direction, on up the Gros Vent Road. I pulled over when I could and called, but saw nothing.

Finally, back at camp, I put a water bottle, some sandwiches, my jacket, my compass, and some matches into my day pack and headed back out of the campground. I parked right across the road at the trailhead and started hiking up the Atherton Ridge Trail, which went straight up the big ridge right above the lake.

I knew the likelihood of finding Diggs in this big wild country was small, but maybe I'd run across someone who had seen him, at least. And this was the general direction I thought I'd heard the woodknocking and barking coming from last night—or had it been a dream?

The trail quickly climbed from the valley, and I was soon on the ridge above the lake. The views were spectacular, and I could finally see the Tetons—the Grand Teton and Teewinot and all the others piercing the sky. I stopped to catch my breath, then continued onward.

The trail went through a mix of pines, aspens, and open space with sagebrush and wildflowers, primarily yellow asters and blue daisies. It was beautiful, though my pant cuffs were soaking wet from all the moisture still on the tall grasses. It seemed like I was the only one on the trail, which didn't surprise me, given the rains.

I stopped about every fifty feet and called for Diggs, but I really didn't expect to see him. At this point, I was feeling like he must be lost to stay out so long.

After a mile or so, I decided to hike up onto a small ridge to see if I could better scope out the country ahead of me. Once up there, I noticed a thick stand of pine over to the northwest a little, and for some reason I decided to go check it out.

Soon there, I walked around, looking for Diggs, but found nothing. I did find a four-point set of deer antlers, probably shed that spring from a small buck. I got my bearings visually, checked my compass, and took off cross-country for another ridge that looked to be about a half-mile off.

Maybe, with some elevation, I could spot him, if he were hanging around up here, which I doubted. But a good search would mean one less place to look, at least.

I climbed and climbed, then sat down on top of the ridge and ate a PBJ sandwich and drank some water. I wanted to keep my strength up, as I suspected it would be a long day. These ridges were not timbered at all, but were rather grass covered, so they made good lookout points.

I sat there for a long time, calling and scanning with my binoculars, looking for any kind of anomaly in the landscape that could be a black and white dog. I knew I would only see a speck from up there, but if it moved, that would be a good enough sign.

Finally, after a half-hour, I decided to head back over to the trail. Even with a compass, I didn't want to get lost, though the landscape here had lots of landmarks. I was half enjoying the hike, it was such beautiful country, but the pallor of Diggs being lost hung over everything like a dark cloud.

I decided to take a shortcut that would bypass the first ridge I'd come over and take me directly to the trail. I could see from my vantage point that it led through another stand of thick forest, but there was no way I could get lost, as the forest was surrounded by grassy meadows, all with good vantage points.

As I entered the stand of forest, I immediately felt the temperature change. This wasn't anything unusual, as stands of timber create islands of temperature differentials, but along with the coolness, I noticed that everything was very quiet.

Now, anyone who's read much about Bigfoot will be familiar with the concept that an area can become very still when Bigfoot is about. Crickets stop rubbing their legs together and sit still, birds fall silent, and even frogs are quiet. The effect has been described as being like a tomb, so one has to suspect that it's somewhat disconcerting.

I had never experienced this before, and my brain tried to interpret it as the forest being stuffy, but when I stopped to figure it out, I realized everything suddenly felt very oppressive. The stillness was like a cloud of fog hanging over everything.

The only way I can really describe it is that it was like that pause after lightning strikes nearby and before you actually hear the thunder. You anticipate something a little fearfully, but in this case, I had no idea what I was anticipating.

I almost turned around, but it just didn't register that this was the very thing I'd heard about from many of my fishing clients, often right before they'd had a Bigfoot encounter. I just wasn't on the Bigfoot page right then, I was thinking about Diggs.

I continued walking, kind of tiptoeing almost as if in a cathedral. The forest was just so still. And then, there it was—in a small clearing, hanging on the branch of a tree—something red and looking totally out of place.

I walked over and took Diggs' collar, the one I'd bought him in Pinedale, off the limb. It was unbuckled—not torn or cut—but neatly unbuckled and hung on the tree.

I was puzzled. What was his collar doing way out here, off the beaten path, hanging from a tree limb? It wasn't like he'd caught it on the limb and pulled it off, as the limb was a good four feet off the ground, way higher than Diggs. Had he tried to climb the tree, maybe chasing a bear, and caught his collar going up or down?

I examined the tree for hair or any kind of clue, but I just didn't see how a dog could get up that high. There weren't enough limbs to climb up there, and Diggs couldn't jump that high.

And as I stood there, totally stunned by my discovery, the sense of oppression seemed even stronger—and darker, if I could explain it that way. It felt strange, and I began to feel that very same kind of fear I'd experienced back when night hiking, that sense of flight or fight, but not like you would feel if encountering a bear, but rather more like if you'd seen something so mysterious and frightening your mind couldn't process it.

I put the collar in my pocket and turned back—and that's when I heard it—a quiet sort of whining, the kind of sound that would come from a very tired and frightened animal.

I turned, and there, in the clearing behind me, stood Diggs.

30. Hot Diggity Diggs

. . . .

Diggs looked tired and despairing, if dogs can despair, and he was covered with dried reddish mud. He slowly wagged his tail, as if glad to see me, but not wanting to expend the energy it would take to really wag.

I picked him up and turned to go back. I went quickly to the edge of the trees, set him down, put his collar back on him, and clipped on the leash. We could make much better time if I didn't carry him, and I felt a strong urge to leave as quickly as possible.

He followed along, but slowly and as if he had no energy, so I again picked him up. At this point, I just wanted to get away from the strange overpowering silence.

I practically ran, Diggs bouncing up and down in my arms. After awhile, I had to put him back down and let him follow along, as he was just too heavy.

We were maybe a half-mile from the trees, heading back up the ridge I'd come down, when I heard a strange sound coming from what seemed to be right where I'd found Diggs. It was rock clacking! Clack, clack—two times—clack, clack—over and over. I sensed it had to be some kind of signal.

I felt panicked. I picked Diggs up again and ran as hard as I could to the top of the ridge, then down the other side, meeting the trail almost exactly where I'd left it.

With the ridge between me and the trees, I felt somewhat safer, though safer from what, I didn't know. But I didn't slack off, I set Diggs back down, trying to pull him along, but again carried him when he seemed too tired to cooperate. But all the way back, I had a feeling I was being followed, or at the least, watched.

Before long, I was down by my truck, exhausted, but safe. I put Diggs into the cab and drove back to camp.

I had to sit at the picnic table for a long time, recovering my breath and strength. I felt totally exhausted. I finally dug out the remainder of the candy from Bear Lake and ate it, which helped my energy levels. I then checked out Diggs, but I couldn't find anything wrong, so I offered him some water and a little jerky. He drank a lot, but wouldn't eat anything, which made me worry.

Finally, I took him down to the lake and washed off the reddish mud. How did he get so muddy, and where did he find red dirt? I was puzzled—all the dirt around camp and even up on the trail was brown or even a little whitish, not red.

My jeans and shirt were stained red from where I'd carried him, and later, after I got home, I ended up having to toss them, as I couldn't get the stain out.

To this day, I have no idea what it was, but something deep inside tells me it was blood. It had that same look to it when it was all said and done, when I was washing Diggs off and when my clothes wouldn't come clean, that look of blood stains.

Had Diggs somehow innocently chased the buffalo to Bigfoot, which had then killed it? Had he somehow played an unwitting part in some strange ritual, maybe a celebration like the natives once had when killing the mighty beasts? It was pure speculation, and I knew Sarah would think I was losing my mind if I even mentioned something so outlandish.

Diggs seemed to have totally lost any interest in running off or chasing, and even though I had him tied to a bush with the long lead, he kept wanting into the truck cab. It was almost as if he didn't feel secure anywhere else.

Finally, I decided to go into Kelly and see if I could find a place to get a few groceries. On my way out, I stopped at the camp host trailer and told Amy I'd found Diggs. She came out and petted him, then remarked on how tired he looked.

"I don't know where he went, but he sure acts different now," I replied.

"Maybe he had a run-in with that bear that's been coming around," Amy answered. She then looked around surreptitiously, as if making sure there was no one around, and said in a low voice, "We're thinking of pulling out. That bear's been here twice and the last time, it tried to break into our trailer."

"What did it do?" I asked. A bear that bold was prime bait for being trapped and relocated.

"It actually didn't do anything," she said. "But both of us saw it looking in at us through the window after dark. It scared the you-know-what out of us."

I paused, then said, "Maybe it was just curious. Did you call a ranger?"

"We did, and they came out, but didn't see it. They said if it keeps coming around they're going to put out a bear trap and move it someplace else."

I had seen such traps. They looked like giant cans on wheels. Bait was put inside and a trap door automatically closed when the bear entered.

Amy looked nervous. "It was actually not like any bear I've ever seen. It was really big, and it had a face that looked almost human. Gives me the chills to think about it. I really think we're going to cut our tour of duty short here. We're volunteers, and there's no reason to stay somewhere you don't want to be, especially if you're afraid for your life."

"It was that scary, eh?" I asked.

"It was."

I got back into my truck, thinking about what I'd heard the previous night and also up on the hill behind the campground not long ago. And what had removed Diggs' collar? I knew it had to be something with hands and an opposable thumb. That would leave only a human—or a Bigfoot.

I wondered if that hadn't really been what the camp hosts had seen, not a bear. Amy had acted like she wanted to tell me more, but then she'd changed her mind.

I drove on down the road to Kelly, seeing a large herd of buffalo out on the sagebrush flats, and once in the town, stumbled onto a sandwich and espresso shop. I went inside and ordered an avocado turkey sandwich with an iced chai, noting the sign that said, "Stay inside if bison in parking lot."

I took it all back out to the truck, where I gave Diggs the turkey off the sandwich, which he gobbled down. He was suddenly famished, and seemed to perk up after that.

I was now feeling more relaxed and even elated that I had Diggs back. There was no way I would ever let him go like that again, not without some serious training and knowing he would stay nearby. I figured that might even take a year or two, but I would rather do that than go through what I'd just been through.

I suddenly wanted to call Sarah. She didn't even know I had a dog. I remembered that Zoey had told me to go to Spencer, Montana, to see the bear dog expert, but I really didn't have any interest in that now. I mostly wanted to go home. I had been on the road for over a month now.

But I still needed to go to Montana. But did I really want to? I could change my mind, I knew that, but I also knew I would regret it later.

I would spend one more night, get rested up, and then decide what to do.

31. Monsters

On the way back, I met several buffalo walking down the middle of the road, as they're prone to do in this area, and as we gingerly and slowly passed them, I noticed that Diggs slid down onto the pickup floor like he was trying to hide.

Whatever had happened that night, he seemed to have gotten the worst of the deal, but at least he didn't seem to have been hurt. I wondered if he would continue to chase, or if he'd been cured.

I felt very lucky to have found him, but I began to wonder if I had somehow been led to him. It didn't really make sense, as I'd heard no voice telling me to go off trail or anything like that, but, in retrospect, once I'd found him, I'd felt a strong sense that something or someone just wanted me to take the dog and leave, to get the heck out of their territory.

Once back at camp, Diggs didn't want to leave the truck, and when I made him get out, he refused to leave my side. I kept him tied, but he tried to follow me as much as the lead would let him, and he seemed very subdued. I wished once again I could ask him what had happened.

And now that we were back, he was again refusing to eat, and even beef jerky couldn't entice him. I can't say this set too well with me, not only because I wanted him to eat, but because it signaled that something was still wrong. Maybe what the camp hosts had seen (and that I suspected had been a Bigfoot, not a bear) was still near camp.

Yes, I did still want to have an encounter, but I didn't want anyone to get hurt, and from the way things felt up in the clearing where I'd found Diggs, I wasn't entirely sure that if there were Bigfoot around, they were pleasantly inclined towards humans.

I decided I would for sure leave the next day. I had pretty much given up on backpacking in Yellowstone, primarily because I couldn't afford the gear, but for some reason I now wasn't feeling bad about that. But I did still need to go on up to Montana. Even if I didn't go Bigfooting up there, I had another mission to fulfill, one that was much more personal than the topic of Bigfoot.

I sat on the picnic table, my legs dangling off the side, thinking about everything. Diggs was curled up under the table, looking miserable and unhappy. I decided it was time to leave.

I could spend another night and possibly have a Bigfoot encounter—maybe whatever it was that had taken Digg's collar off would come for a visit. Or maybe it wasn't a Bigfoot at all, but rather was a person out hiking who had seen the dog and, thinking he was lost, had tried to catch him, inadvertently pulling his collar off and then hanging it on the tree.

The forest where I'd found him had felt really strange, but who's to say that wasn't just my own emotional perceptions and not reality at all? And the rock clacking could've been squirrels or marmots or something like that. I knew that Bigfoot wasn't necessarily the source of everything strange that happens in the woods.

I loaded up my camp chair and stove, then took down the tarp and got Diggs into the truck. It just felt like it was time to go, and his unhappy behavior underscored my decision. And what if we did have a Bigfoot visit us that night? It would just serve to scare the little dog even more, and probably me, too. And it seemed like I'd be better off not having an encounter at all than having one like that.

I stopped by the camp host trailer to say goodbye to Amy, but no one was there. I knew they, too, would soon leave. As it was, most of the campground was empty, partially due to the weather.

I drove on to Kelly and decided to see if I could get ahold of Sarah to let her know where I was going, but her phone was turned off. I left a message, knowing she was still in the Piceance Basin with no cell service.

I got to the intersection with the main highway and turned north. I could now see the Tetons in all their glory, and the sight lifted my spirits. Diggs also seemed to be feeling better, and I gave him a few dog biscuits, which he quickly munched down.

As we drove along, I thought about all that had happened back at Slide Lake, and I wondered again if my perceptions had possibly led me astray. I was aware that the human imagination was a powerful thing, in both good and bad ways—the good being that it makes us creative, and the bad being that it sets us up for scenarios that aren't necessarily real. Had my feelings in the woods above Slide Lake been the latter?

I recalled a conversation I once had with a friend over a campfire up on the Frying Pan River, near Basalt, Colorado. We'd managed to scare ourselves talking about Bigfoot until we imagined we could hear one in the bushes. It turned out to be a deer, and our conversation had turned to a discussion of what makes something scary.

This, in turn, led to talk about what made something a monster, as opposed to just another strange creature on Planet Earth. What characteristics did something need before we would be terrified of it?

It was a fun conversation, and if I recall correctly, we decided that the most terrifying monsters had the following characteristics:

They were human-like or had a human element, like human eyes. Playing with our associations of creatures that were like us yet that wanted to kill us made them scarier than a non-human creature. Also, things that are human-like garner our sympathies, yet don't, leaving us confused, which adds to the terror.

It has to be plausible. Something that defies the laws of gravity might scare us at first, but we know deep inside it's not real. But something that's plausible and really could exist is much scarier.

It has to be mysterious and hard to explain. It helps a lot if it hides in the deep dark forest at night and we can't see it. This plays on our fears of the unknown, and since we're very visual animals, it also plays into our greatest weakness.

It has to be intelligent. That way, survival becomes a test of will and smarts. It helps if it's intelligent but also malevolent and can't be reasoned with.

You don't know how to deal with it. Feeling helpless adds to feeling terrified. It makes it even scarier if it's stealthy.

But for me, what makes something really terrifying is when you can't escape.

I pondered all this darkness while some of the most beautiful mountains in the world—the Tetons— could be seen out my window, and I acknowledged that leaving Slide Lake had probably been a good thing, even if just to get away from my own imagination. But Diggs' behavior did affirm that it wasn't all in my mind, and for me, then and there, escaping was the better part of valor.

We drove on, and the further we got from Slide Lake, the better both of us seemed to feel. I stopped in Colter Lake Village and got us each a hamburger, which Diggs wolfed down like he'd been starving, then I took him for a walk on the shores of Jackson Lake, wondering if it, too, like Bear Lake, had a supposed lake monster.

We continued on and were soon in Yellowstone. I thought again about my plans to backpack into the corner of the park, but now I just wanted to get up to Montana. I was running out of time and money.

Finally, as the sun was setting, we reached the town of Gardiner—we were finally in Montana. I was exhausted, so I decided to get a motel, the first on my entire trip. Now that I would soon be heading back home, I knew I had enough money, but just barely.

I was hoping for a cheap Motel 6, but no luck, so I checked into a Super 8 that would take pets, took Diggs in, and was soon enjoying my first hot shower in what felt like forever, nothing further from my mind than Bigfoot.

32. Courage

The next day, I took Diggs for a short walk, then we were again on our way. We saw a small herd of mountain sheep near the road, and I was happy to see Diggs watching them like a normal dog would, on full alert, with that "Oh boy, chasable wildlife!" look.

Before long, we were in the Paradise Valley, one of the most beautiful stretches of road in Montana, or anywhere, for that matter, with the massive Absaroka Mountains on the east and the Gallatins on the west.

I felt a comfortable sense of familiarity—I had spent a lot of time here, mostly fishing the Yellowstone, and I was close to my destination, which was high in the Bridger Mountains, just north of the Gallatins.

Before long, I was in Livingston, a town that's always been on my list of places I could live—at least in the summer, as its winter winds are infamous. But it has trains, which I love.

I now had to make a decision. My rendezvous high in the Bridgers could be reached in two ways—I could go north from Livingston and circle around into the mountains on a back highway, or I could go over Bozeman Pass and come up from their west side.

Having a good friend in Bozeman I hadn't seen in some time, I decided on the latter. I would go see my old fishing buddy James, who owns a fly-fishing guide business and has a store near downtown Bozeman, where he sells fishing gear and gives introductory lessons.

I sometimes worked with James, coming up into various parts of Montana to guide, mostly on the the Big Hole and Yellowstone Rivers. James was my Montana connection, and it would be good to go see him and make plans for next year's season, assuming he wasn't out guiding.

I arrived at his store in Bozeman and lucked out. James was surprised to see me, and he liked the "I Shot the Sheriff" sticker on my topper and gave me a couple with fishing slogans to add to it—my favorite said, "Women Love Me, Fish Fear Me." We soon ended up down at the Montana Ale Works while Diggs slept in the cab of the truck.

It was good to see my old friend—we went way back—and we got caught up over a few rounds of, appropriately enough, a locally brewed ale called "Trout Slayer." We then traded fishing stories, known by some as lies.

James invited me to stay the night, and he and his wife, Khaki, have a big fenced back yard, where I let Diggs out to play with their yellow lab, Honey. Remembering what Zoey had said about bear dogs being aggressive with other dogs, I was at first nervous, but the two got along great.

After dinner, James' wife went upstairs to read, leaving the two of us to our own devices. We sat on his back deck, and Diggs lay by my feet, worn out from playing. I suspected the little dog was still trying to regain energy from his escapade.

James and I had talked some through the years about Bigfoot, and he'd partaken of several of my campfire dinners and heard plenty of stories, but he always told me it was just folklore, and I probably shouldn't get too hung up on ever seeing one. I knew he didn't believe they existed and thought my search was a fool's quest, but I didn't care, we were still the best of friends.

We had spent part of the previous evening talking about my current Bigfoot expedition, if one wanted to call it that, but he also knew that wasn't why I was going up in the Bridgers.

James suddenly seemed pensive, and after he studied me for a moment, he asked, "Rusty, you're here to go up to Fairy Lake, aren't you?"

I nodded yes, saying nothing, sipping my beer.

"I know," he continued. "It's that time of year. Doesn't it get better, though, each year? I mean, they say time heals all wounds, or does it help at all?"

By now, I myself was pretty socked under from the alcohol and feeling emotional, as I suspected James was, too.

All I could say was, "Yeah, time does help, but not enough. It's just something I'll probably need to do for awhile."

"Well, at least I get to see you more often that way," James replied. We sat in silence, then he finally showed me to my room. That night, I slept like a baby, no thought of Bigfoot, Diggs snoring on a rug by my bed.

The next morning, we said our goodbyes after a few cups of coffee and some pancakes, and I knew it would be awhile before I saw James again—probably early next summer, unless he were to first come down my way.

He seemed overly quiet, and I knew he was thinking of my mission to Fairy Lake—either that, or he was a bit hungover.

Diggs and I were soon on our way up the road into the Bridgers, which was also the road to the local ski area, Bridger Bowl. I could see the tall peaks towering above, but they soon disappeared as we drove up Bridger Canyon Road.

It was over 20 miles to the turnoff to Fairy Lake, all good paved highway, but the six miles or so on up to the lake was an entirely different matter, rough in places with high clearance necessary. We bounced along, Diggs hanging his nose out the window, smelling the air with curiosity.

We wound though beautiful stands of pine and aspens dotted with open grassy meadows filled with wildflowers—purple lupine and larkspur mixed with yellow mules' ears and dried grasses.

I loved the Bridgers for their quiet beauty. They were nothing like the spectacular Tetons, but seemed much more homey and accessible. And I loved Fairy Lake—it was like an emerald gem set under the flanks of Sacagawea Peak. I had never hiked to the nearby smaller Elf Lake, which I'd heard was also like a jewel.

We eventually arrived at the Fairy Lake Campground, and I found a great camp spot. There were only a few tents around, presumably of hikers, as there was no one there.

I got out my camp stove and made some more coffee, feeling pretty tired, probably the effects of the previous day. After giving Diggs some kibble, I took him for a short hike on the trail that circles the lake.

Above us stood Sacagawea, and next to it, one of my favorite peaks, Naya Nuki. I had a special affinity for Naya Nuki, primarily for the story behind its name.

Naya Nuki was an 11-year-old Shoshoni girl, kidnapped by Mandan Indians at the same time as Sacagawea. Sacagawea remained in captivity, eventually guiding the Lewis and Clark expedition across Montana in 1805, but Naya Nuki escaped and then travelled alone across North Dakota into Montana, back to her home.

When Sacagawea finally arrived back in her home region with the Lewis and Clark bunch, she was reunited with Naya Nuki, their embrace described by Meriwether Lewis.

Many consider Naya Nuki's story to be the more courageous of the two, as she travelled alone for 1,000 miles across very rugged and wild country with only the food she could find herself, swimming some pretty big rivers, and outwitting predators.

I sat down on a big rock and let Diggs wade out into the lake, still on his leash, while I thought of Naya Nuki. Her story embodied a desire for freedom that overpowered any thoughts of security or safety. Pretty amazing for an 11-year-old, in my book.

I then thought back of the many recent nights I'd been afraid of my own shadow, and I felt humbled. I knew that the young native girl had far more things to be afraid of than I'd ever had, and I wondered what it had been like for her, journeying alone through country far wilder than any place I'd ever been.

Tonight would be my last night camping, and I vowed to make the most of it. I would refuse to worry about anything. For all practical purposes, my Bigfoot mission had ended at Slide Lake, and my mission here was of a different nature—and I was almost done.

By tomorrow afternoon, I would be on my way back home, such that it was, and I would see Sarah in a mere couple of days. I had decided not to tell her about Diggs, but to leave it as a surprise—a good surprise I hoped, seeing how the little dog was such a handful. Time would tell, I figured, as I turned and led the little wet dog back to camp for the night.

33. The Rendezvous

. . . .

I was up very early the next morning.

It was time to complete my mission, the last thing I wanted to do before going home. After a quick breakfast, I put water bottles, sandwiches, and dog biscuits in my daypack, and Diggs and I started up a trail I'd walked many times before, though mostly in happier times.

We were going to climb Sacagawea.

By Colorado standards, which I was used to, having climbed a number of that state's Fourteeners, Sac was almost more of a hill at 9,665 feet. But the steepness of the hiking trail to the top, plus all the scree, made for a stiff climb, even at a short 2.2 miles one-way.

I hoped to be on top before noon, some 2,000 feet above where I stood, before distant clouds moved in, some possibly bearing lightning.

I had Diggs on his long leash, but it was a pain, trying to lead him up the narrow trail. Every so often, he would stop unexpectedly to sniff something, and I would almost trip over or step on him.

I hadn't seen anyone else on the trail, even though it was a popular climb. As we slowly climbed up a long narrow valley, the evergreens gradually became more sparse. A number of snow-fed streams fed stands of red paintbrush, white lilies, and purple bluebells.

In spite of crossing several debris fields, we were finally making good time, Diggs finally hiking instead of sniffing, gradually climbing what had now become a steep trail into a glacial cirque above timberline. I could see a series of narrow switchbacks going up a headwall above us, and huffing and puffing, we were soon to a saddle where a weathered sign read, "Turn L for Sacagawea Peak, R for Hardscrabble Peak."

I stopped, the view overwhelming me. We stood on a high ridge that made up part of the Bridger Divide, and I could see an incredible morass of mountains in the distance. The trail now turned to the south, following along a ridge that led to the summit.

The views of the Bridgers were bottomless, heady, and I was glad I'd kept Diggs on his leash, as I could see a small group of shaggy white mountain goats in a gully not far below us. They stood and watched us for a moment, then slipped away into the morning shadow.

A few more zigzags, and we were on top. The wind had picked up, and I could see ripening fields of wheat far below.

We were standing on the highest peak of the Bridger Range, and as I turned in a 360-degree circle, I could see the Gallatin and Madison Ranges to the south, the Big Belts to the north, the Elkhorns and Tobacco Roots to the west, and the Crazies to the east. It was an unforgettable view.

I turned and unclipped Diggs from his lead. For some reason, it suddenly felt wrong, keeping him tied to me—he was a free spirit, just as I was. He stood at my side, making no motion to leave. It was as if he, too, was overwhelmed by the vista before us.

It all seemed overwhelming, and I sat on a big chunk of gray rock to ponder the insignificant yet magnificent feeling it all gave me. I wished Sarah were here so I could ask her about the geology, as the gray rocks looked very old, like rocks she'd shown me in Colorado and Utah. I picked up a small sample and stuck it in my pocket—I would ask her when I got home.

But now it was time for my ritual, the same one I'd performed every year since my best friend Danny had died, killed two days after he and I had climbed this very same peak, five years ago. It was time for my rendezvous with the specter of his death.

I stood and dropped five brand new pennies into a small pile behind a large rock a bit away from where people would be likely to see them. The pennies I'd left from each previous year were still there, one penny for each year since Danny's death.

Next year, I would come and leave six, and maybe, just maybe when the pile grew to where it could be seen shining in the sun from far below, maybe then I would have some closure and be able to abandon the climb, though I hoped it would come sooner.

I stood there, thinking of Danny and how close we'd been, of how much he'd meant to me, like a little brother through much of my life until he was suddenly gone, and I still felt guilt over his death.

He'd wanted me to go climbing with him the day he fell, but I'd been busy, teaching a fishing class for James. Danny went without me and never returned, and I often wonder if he might've been OK if I'd gone along.

Danny loved kids, though he didn't have any of his own. He'd graduated from Montana State University with a degree in education and got a job teaching fifth grade, and his students loved him.

Danny and I were, in many ways, complete opposites, but I think that was part of what made us such good friends. He liked to hang out and joke around with his buddies, while I was much more solitary and was happiest when out alone, fishing. I'll never forget his infectious laugh—no matter how down you felt, he could turn you around.

But the one thing we had in common was our love of nature, and that love led us to hike and climb together whenever we could, which wasn't often enough, with him in Montana and me in Colorado. But Sac had been our last outing together.

I wanted to cry, but didn't. Last time I was here, I had cried plenty, but this time, things felt better, and I knew Danny wouldn't want me to mourn him any more.

Across a long narrow ridge stood Naya Nuki Peak, and I thought again of the young native girl and the heartbreak she must've had, being kidnapped and losing her family. I vowed to do better, to be happier, if just for the sake of Danny's memory.

Just then, the sun broke through the clouds, a beam shining directly on the pile of pennies. Though I'm not much of one for signs and portents, it made me feel that somehow all would be well, that I was finally healing.

It was time to go. I turned and started back down, Diggs never straying from my heels all the way back, even with no lead to constrain him. He didn't even pay any attention to the mountain goats as we again passed them, and I began to think maybe he was a changed dog, just as climbing Sac that day had changed me.

34. Freedom

. . . .

The day was almost done, evening was falling, and I still sat at the picnic table, next to my truck at Fairy Lake. I was tired, but something was holding me back. I wanted nothing more than to be on the road home, but yet I couldn't seem to get up the energy to get up and leave.

Diggs lay by me, and I could tell he was very tired, so I put him into the truck cab with some biscuits. For some reason, I needed to stay a little longer—maybe I just needed more closure. I just wasn't ready to go, in spite of my strong desire to leave.

I finally got up and put a few sticks in a nearby fire pit. It was almost dark, and I decided I'd make a little fire, one that would burn out quickly, but something to light up the oncoming darkness until I could make myself leave. I then sat back down.

All of a sudden, for no reason and with no warning, the hair on my neck stood straight up. This is an automatic response from the days we had hair, an attempt to make ourselves look larger when in danger. I was suddenly afraid to even turn around, as I knew there was something straight behind me. I was terrified.

I sat there, stone scared, and something came up right next to me. I was afraid to even turn my head to look at it—I was literally scared stiff, as I knew it was not human.

I felt something on my shoulder, and it squeezed a bit, then let go. I could now see from the corner of my eye that it was a huge hand, and it was almost like a friendly squeeze, but I was too scared to do anything but sit there staring into the fire. I wish now I had turned and acknowledged it, at least, but I didn't.

It then turned and walked back into the forest, leaving a musky smell behind. By the time I came out of shock, I stood up and turned around, and all I could see was this massive creature slipping into the trees—walking on two legs.

It left me with a feeling of fear and affirmation, and I'm not one for mystical stuff, but it almost seemed like it was telling me everything was OK. Maybe I just projected that, but it really felt that was the message there. Call me nuts if you want, and I'll probably agree with you.

I thought again of the words I'd read at the folklore library:

Bigfoot shows himself to those individuals who he feels are ready to see him.

Did I actually see a Bigfoot? I'm not sure, but I did see what looked like a big hairy hand, and I definitely felt it on my shoulder. And when I finally did get up the courage to turn and look, I swore I saw a giant shadowy figure slipping into the forest.

Could I prove any of this? No, but I no longer cared. I no longer felt the need to prove anything to anyone, for I knew in my heart what I'd just experienced.

Could it have been a hallucination or a dream? I would say no, but I can't prove it wasn't. But to me, it was very real, and the existence of Bigfoot was no longer a question. I knew it existed, and I knew I had somehow been recognized as a friend.

The suddenness of it all was overwhelming. I sat there in shock, until finally a wave of warmth spread over me, just like one would feel if they dipped themselves into a hot spring.

I then felt a peace, a feeling that my mission, such that it had been, was complete, and that I could now return home. I no longer had anything to prove to anyone, and somehow trying to convince the world that Bigfoot actually existed seemed unimportant and even frivolous.

I thought of all the nervous nights I'd spent and how hard I'd been on myself over these fears, and it all seemed to fade into the dusk.

And I thought of my entire trip evolving around the concept of a meeting, the idea that I would end my journey with a rendezvous with Danny's death on the heights of Sacagawea, trying yet again to make sense of it all.

I had never dreamed that the real rendezvous would be like this. I had completely given up on ever having a Bigfoot encounter—and yet, this had seemed like much more than any encounter I could have ever imagined happening. Yet to simply call it an encounter seemed to somehow diminish its power.

Slowly, I stood, got into the cab, gave Diggs a pat on the head, then turned my truck towards home.

I drove and drove, finally pulling over near Jackson to sleep some. I was in a small forest, but it never occurred to me to be afraid, and I slept well, continuing my journey home the next day.

Since that night up at Fairy Lake, that feeling of peace has stayed with me, and I consider it a very special gift, one that I probably didn't deserve, but one I will gladly accept and hold close forever in gratitude.

I have often wondered if that sense of peace I felt up in the High Uintas wasn't maybe a similar thing—maybe there was a Bigfoot nearby, and it somehow engendered that same feeling.

I'm no longer afraid to be out at night alone, though I still exercise caution where there might be bears or mountain lions. But my deepest fears are gone.

And from now on, I'll be chasing after fish rather than chasing after Bigfoot—but if the Big Guy comes to pay me another visit, I won't mind a bit.

Afterword

· ·

After I returned home, Sarah and I found a nice little cabin to rent on the edge of an aspen forest a few miles from Steamboat Springs. There was a small lake nearby, but I was pretty sure it had no lake monsters.

We moved our little camp trailer there, where Sarah fixed it up as her home office, immediately decorating it with rocks she'd collected through the years. I figured if a big wind ever came through, we didn't have to worry about it blowing away, that's for sure.

And yes, all her trying to teach me something about geology did pay off—the rock sample I brought back from Sacagawea was limestone and among some of the older rocks on the planet—Devonian and 360 million years old.

I hadn't forgotten Tim, and I occasionally sent him photos of Diggs. One day, he finally sent a photo back, one of a scruffy little yellow dog his mom and dad had gotten him at the shelter in Jackson. His name was—oddly enough— Diggs the Second, or Diggs for short. Sarah and I had a good laugh over that.

We did eventually hear back from the people in Spencer, and they had tracked down who our Diggs was. He hadn't been stolen, like I'd suspected, but had been purchased from a Montana breeder by a woman who had died a couple of months later. Since her husband was on the road a lot, he gave the dog to her brother, who then gave Diggs to Tim. The people in Spencer felt we would be within our rights to keep the dog, as did we.

Sarah didn't really care for the name Diggs, feeling it wasn't worthy for a dog with such an esteemed lineage, so he became Vladimir, or Vladdie. Since he was from a Finnish lineage, I wasn't surprised—though I had figured she would name him something like Mikko or Frederik or even Chinook or Atlas. But Vladdie didn't stick, and he eventually went back to being Diggs.

Because the instinct is actually genetic, Diggs will always be a hunter, but I think his experience there in the Gros Vent taught him to be prudent about what he hunts, as he now won't leave our sides when hiking. But he was indeed quite the hunter, as we found after he chased down and captured our hearts.

And through time, we found Diggs to be the opposite in some ways of what the woman had told Zoey—he was actually very easy to train, very loyal and protective, and very sociable with other dogs. And when Zoey and Tom came to visit, Diggs became infatuated with Zadie, much to everyone's amusement and delight.

As for Bigfoot, well, Sarah still doesn't believe, even after hearing my story. She says that Bigfoot represents the unknown within ourselves, as well as our attempts, as urban creatures who were once wild, to recover our wildness.

And to her, the Bigfoot meme also signals a deep need in humans to recapture the hero quest and all it entails, something once satisfied by our original wanderings, as well as the tales told by the master storytellers of old around the campfire, who are now all gone, pretty much leaving us on our own.

Whatever, is all I can say, though I try to be nice about it. To me, there's no question that Bigfoot is a real, living, breathing creature, elusive as he or she may be. Like the paranormal explanations, I put no credence in the psychological ones. And I'm sure Bigfoot would laugh if he could listen in.

But if you decide to go chasing after Bigfoot, all I can say is to be prepared for anything, because I can pretty much guarantee it won't turn out like you might expect.

You see, I believe those big Bigfoot feet march to the beat of a different drummer, a drummer our human ears can only hear when we are very still and very quiet and very humble.

All my best and stay wild, —Rusty

About the Author

Rusty Wilson grew up in the state of Washington, in the heart of Bigfoot country. He didn't know a thing about Bigfoot until he got lost at the age of six and was then found and subsequently adopted by a kindly Bigfoot family. He lived with them until he was 16, when they finally gave up on ever socializing him into Bigfoot ways (he hated garlic and pancakes, refused to sleep in a nest, wouldn't hunt wild pigs, and on top of it all, his feet were small).

His Bigfoot family then sent him off to Evergreen State College in nearby Olympia, thinking it would be liberal enough to take care of a kid with few redeeming qualities, plus they liked the thick foliage around the college and figured Rusty could live there, saving them money for housing.

At Evergreen, Rusty studied wildlife biology, eventually returning to the wilds, after first learning to read and write and regale everyone with his wild tales.

He eventually became a fly-fishing guide, and during his many travels in the wilds, he collected stories from others who have had contact with Bigfoot, also known as Sasquatch. Because of his background, Rusty is considered to be the world's Bigfoot expert (at least so by himself, if not by anyone else). He's spent many a fun evening around campfires with his clients, telling stories. Some of those clients had some pretty good stories of their own.

Rusty's books are available as ebooks and in print and audio form at Amazon.com.

Suspend disbelief and go on a road trip with a Bigfoot in Rusty's book, "The Bigfoot Runes," an adventure like none you'll ever see again. One reviewer (unclesquirrel) says: "If you are a enthusiast of bigfoot this book is a great read! This author is a masterful story teller! I know I would love to sit around a campfire with him!"

You can follow and communicate with Rusty at his blog at rustybigfoot.blogspot.com. And check out Bigfoot Head-quarters at yellowcatbooks.com.

Also, you'll enjoy "The Ghost Rock Cafe" by Chinle Miller, a Bigfoot mystery. Also available at the above websites.

Whether you're a Bigfoot believer or not, we hope you enjoyed this book, and we know you'll enjoy Rusty's many others, the first of which is "Rusty Wilson's Bigfoot Campfire Stories."

www.ingramcontent.com/pod-product-compliance
Lightning Source LLC
Chambersburg PA
CBHW051130020726
47501CB00005B/1435